"Go with it..."

Pulling his tie loose, Dalton left it around his neck as he flicked first his vest then his shirt open. They landed on the floor beside his jacket. He was tan, smooth-skinned and defined in a way that made Cass hunger to run her hands over his body.

Cass couldn't look away from him. He owned the moment, so compelling and utterly sexual in a way she'd never experienced.

He surged to his feet, hips rolling and thrusting in time to the music. The way he moved had to be illegal in twenty-seven states. Maybe twenty-eight. Or forty.

Glancing up, she was stunned to find him watching her.

Eyes brimming with something primitive and dark, he never looked away from Cass as he grabbed Gwen's hand and guided her through removing his belt. He stalked around them. One wide hand moved around Cass's waist to feed the belt across her lower hips. Dalton gripped each end and leaned back, forcing Cass to arch her spine. Dropping the belt, he grabbed her hips and moved against her, and her mind went totally blank.

The only thing she could manage was conjuring images of Dalton naked, in bed, pulling some of the same moves. Cass closed her eyes.

Her first inclination was to regain control.

But she had *earned* this... And it would only be one night.

A night no one would, or could, ever know about...

Blaze

Dear Reader,

Welcome to the world of Pleasure Before Business and, more specifically, Beaux Hommes, the most exclusive all-male revue in the Pacific Northwest. The men are hot both on the stage and between the sheets. Their lives are just the way they like them. As the most popular thing to happen in Seattle once the sun goes down, things just don't get much better than this. But for all they love to please, they have hopes and dreams much bigger than Wednesday through Saturday night work schedules, screaming female fans and G-strings. The one thing they never banked on? Love itself.

The idea for the stripper series was born when this criminally sexy hero started whispering to me about what it was like to be trapped in one career that strictly pays the bills so he could pursue his real dream. He talked about paying his dues, fighting his way to the top, craving that elusive thing: respect. The one thing he was certain of? There was absolutely no time for romance or, heaven forbid, *love*. He had plans!

Poor guy should never, *ever* have thrown down that particular gauntlet.

I hope you'll find a few laughs, a little heartache and a huge amount of redemption in this story. I know, as I wrote it, that I learned what it meant to really root for your own characters' happy endings.

Fondly,

Kelli Ireland

Stripped Down

—

Kelli Ireland

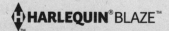

HARLEQUIN® BLAZE™

Recycling programs
for this product may
not exist in your area.

ISBN-13: 978-0-373-79818-6

STRIPPED DOWN

Copyright © 2014 by Denise Tompkins

Printed in U.S.A.

www.Harlequin.com

ABOUT THE AUTHOR

From stable hand to a name on the door of a corporate American office, Kelli Ireland has been many things. (Never a waitress, however. Thank-you cards for her sparing the unsuspecting public from this catastrophe can be sent in care of her agent.) Writing has always been her passion, though. And writing romance? An absolute dream come true. Her theory is that a kiss should be meaningful regardless of length, a hero can say as much with a well-written look as he can with a long-winded paragraph and heroines are meant to hold their own. She's no Cinderella, and Shakespeare wrote the only *Romeo and Juliet,* so Kelli sticks to women who can save themselves and tortured heroes who are loath to let them.

Kelli and her husband live in the South, where all foods are considered fry-able and bugs die only to be reborn in bloodsucking triplicate. Visit her onlne at kelliireland.com anytime.

To the only man to ever hold my heart in his hands.

1

FEET PROPPED ON the low windowsill and ankles crossed, Cass Jameson focused on her toes. Rather, the polish on her toe*nails*. The electric blue polish, "Ogre the Top Blue" courtesy of OPI, was the only color in her otherwise staid corporate attire. She loved the color with an unholy passion, but it also served a purpose.

After her environmental engineering firm, Preservations, celebrated its first full year of operating in the black, Cass had treated herself to three indulgent days at a luxury spa. She'd purchased the nail polish before she left as a constant reminder she could, *would,* make Preservations a success. That trip had been the first time she'd allowed herself to breathe in more than three years. Now, eleven months later, she was holding her breath again.

So much hinged on the incoming email from the Environmental Protection Agency. Preservations had been awarded the contracts for establishing rainwater runoff and soil erosion at the proposed site of the elite Chok Resort on Lake Washington. She and her team had busted their asses for months to create long-term, environmentally sound solutions. They were due to present their plan to the resort's builder, Sovereign Developments, in under a week. Sovereign's board of directors, made up of old men with even older money, wanted a cheap fix to the runoff and erosion problems, but they also wanted the project endorsed as green construction for tax purposes and public support. She couldn't deliver on the former. The latter? She had it covered in spades.

But *only if* the EPA signed off on Preservations' plans. If it did, Sovereign would be hard-pressed to reject her proposal. She'd have the backing she needed to persuade the tight-assed CEO to move forward. Probably. Maybe. God, she hoped so.

A kernel of dread, her constant companion as this deal had been negotiated, threatened to erupt. Pressing her fist into her diaphragm, she forced her breathing to slow. Just once she'd be the emotionless Ice Princess her competitors accused her of being. Ironic that her father, David Jameson, was heralded for his cold-blooded business dealings while her peers and competing engineering firms lobbed it at her as an insult.

A seagull rode a thermal by the fourth-floor window, drawing her attention. Low-hanging clouds shrouded the Seattle skyline and blanketed pedestrians below in heavy mist. Behind her, her laptop chimed.

Such a soft, innocuous sound, that, the herald of her fate. Her fingers curled around the armrests of her chair, but she didn't drop her feet or face the monitor. Not yet.

She'd known securing this location had been a good strategy. It hadn't come cheap, but it positioned Preservations close to the downtown business district and near contractors. Signing the five-year lease had been a calculated risk.

"Greater the risk, greater the reward," she murmured. *Provided the risk pays out.* Her father's baritone echoed through her head, unwelcome. Particularly now.

Muffled voices hummed as the hive of employees gathered outside her door.

Her office door handle rattled as the door opened. She should really call maintenance, have them fix that.

"You didn't read it, did you?" Gwen's tone was neutral, guarded even.

Shoving her feet into her high heels, Cass swiveled toward her business partner and best friend. Everything they'd worked for—all the long nights studying, the family expectations, the sexist remarks of her peers, the casually exchanged conversation between competitors that she and Gwen were destined to fail as women in a man's world—it all came down to this. "Tell me the EPA cleared us to move forward with the Sovereign project. Tell me Preservations is going to be solvent for years to come because our proposal was accepted. Tell me we can hold Sovereign's board to their agreement to move forward with our solutions if we could get absolute EPA support. Say the words, Gwennie."

The stunning petite blonde propped a hip on the corner of Cass's desk. "You need to breathe."

She shook her head. "I can't. Not yet. You know how I get."

"You're right. I do. Here's a news flash, Cass. Your biggest character flaw? You're always expecting the worst. Negative Nancies aren't attractive."

"Negative Nancies?" One corner of her mouth curled up. "This is business. Being an emotionally reserved pessimist has kept us afloat."

Gwen's brows drew together in a fierce scowl. "You sound like your father."

A small hitch in Cass's chest made her words raspy. "I'm not my father."

"Then don't be so afraid to express a little emotion. You're not an automaton."

But a lifetime as the oldest child of business magnate David Jameson, a man who valued control above all else, had taught her to smother her reactions. He'd hammered home one thing above all else: to reveal emotion was to reveal weakness, and any opponent worth his salt would use that weakness against her. He'd proved it by using her emotions against her again and again, until all that was left between them was undisguised resentment and, at least on her part, more than a little paranoia.

When she'd founded Preservations, she'd been so concerned about being singled out as Jameson's daughter she'd gone into business under her mother's maiden name—Wheeler. She'd also kept her name buried in the company directory, not touting her partial ownership. Distancing herself from both his name and his expectations had been a matter of self-preservation. She hated him for making it a necessity. She hated him more for continuing to steal moments like this from her.

"Cass?"

Running a hand around the back of her neck, she took a deep breath before looking at Gwen. "I'm working on it."

"You need to have fun, let your hair down, dance on a few tabletops now and then. You're not fooling me."

"I know. Just…update my online dating profile *after* you tell me what the email says, okay?"

"Oh! Can I really update your profile?" Gwen grinned and did a little hip shimmy on the desk.

Cass sighed and pinched the bridge of her nose, closing her eyes for a second. "Why do women who are about to get married always want to hook their friends up?"

"Because it makes us happy to think said friend, singular, is not destined to end up alone with subscriptions to multiple trashy tabloids that she reads aloud to the twenty-seven cats she lives with in an apartment that smells like tuna salad and vapor rub." Gwen never stopped smiling. "Now, if you promise me I can update your profile, I'll tell you what you want to know, since you're not brave enough to read it yourself."

"I promise," Cass said between gritted teeth.

"Deal. The EPA cleared us straight across the board. We're green-lighted to present the solutions to Sovereign Developments and its backers."

"Straight across the board. They accepted everything." Cass whispered the questions, but her intrepid spirit wound through the words so they came out with concrete assurance. Clearing her throat, she rose to her full height and squared her shoulders. The invisible fist that had been strangling her instinctive emotional response relaxed and, without warning, she erupted in a hip-shaking boogie dance, pumping her fists in the air with a scream. Yanking Gwen off the desk, she spun the woman in circles. Shouts and cheers rose outside the office door. Months of hard work and long hours had paid off. "Grab your partners and—"

"If she cries out 'do-si-do,' I'm outta here," someone shouted.

"Funny guy," Cass shouted back, laughing. "Grab your partners and meet us at Bathtub Gin tomorrow night. We can officially afford to say, 'It's on us!'"

Another cheer went up in the hallway, shouts and laughter weaving through the raucous group as everyone took a deep breath.

Cass realized she'd been clutching Gwen's hand hard enough to mottle the woman's skin. Releasing it, she stepped back. "Someday I'm going to get through this without you."

Gwen shut the office door to a chorus of laughter as the group moved off. Turning, she leaned against the nearest bookshelf. "I hope you always need me, Cass."

"I didn't mean…" She ran fingers through her hair, disrupting the smooth chignon. Tucking the loosened pieces in place, she moved to stand over Gwen. In heels, it was easy to dwarf the petite blonde.

"You're looming, love."

"I know." Cass leaned down and kissed the woman's cheek.

"Does this mean I get a rose and you ask me to stay on your island?" Gwen demanded, hands on her hips.

Cass laughed, that kernel of dread morphing into something effervescent and pervasive, something suspiciously akin to hope. It spread through her limbs and left her feeling light and impossibly encouraged. "We now officially have two things to celebrate," she said, letting a slow, seductive smile spread over her face.

Gwen stepped back, smacking into the door. "I know that look. That look says you're going to get me in trouble with Dave. I'm getting married next Saturday, Cass. I can't exactly return the dress, and I want that damn cake. We got a layer of peanut butter and jelly." She slid along the door as Cass stalked forward.

"You're the one who said to live a little."

Gwen shook her head. "*You*. Not me. *You* live a little. I've lived. I'm tired of living. That's why I'm getting married." Her brow furrowed. "That's not what I meant."

"Uh-huh."

"Cass, Dave has specifically forbidden me from getting in over my head, and the expression on your face says you're throwing me in the deep end in a total sink-or-swim, survival-style move."

"Yep." A feral grin tugged at Cass's lips. She adored Dave, but no one would ever truly be good enough for Gwen. It just wasn't possible.

"Swimming?" Gwen tugged at her collar. "I didn't bring my bathing suit."

"*Naked* swimming, Gwen."

A sheen of sweat dotted her friend's upper lip. "N-Naked?"

"As in, without clothes. Yes." Cass reached out and grabbed her best friend's wrist when she reached for the door. "Nope. No bailing. Dave will be fine with this. He's no doubt getting the same treatment. You're not leaving my side until the night's over."

"A bachelorette party?" Gwen gasped.

The sound of surprise struck Cass particularly hard. "You didn't actually think I'd let you get married without a party, did you?"

"What happened to the emotionally suppressed pessimist? I want her back."

"Too bad. You're the one who told me to dance on a few tables. Besides, we still need to have my and Dave's names tattooed on your ass. He gets left and I'll always be right. It's more poetic that way."

"Tattoos?" Gwen squeaked, edging toward the door again.

Cass coughed to cover her laugh. "Truth?"

The smaller woman nodded, wide eyes never leaving Cass's face.

"Nothing's going to happen tonight that you don't want to happen. Period. I've got your back, as always." She arched a brow and slapped a cuff on Gwen's wrist, fastening the other around her own before the other woman could react.

"You let me go right now, Ramona Cassidy Jameson, or I'm calling your father and informing him you're a sexual deviant."

"Stomp your foot and I swear I'll dump your new Mac in the Sound."

Gwen watched her for a minute and then smiled wide. "You would, too. That's one of the reasons I like you so much. You don't take shit from anyone, ever, and you always come out on top."

"Because I fight to get there." Cass grinned down at the vixen latched to her wrist. "Tonight? What you do, I do. That'll keep things from getting too wild."

"Too wild?" Gwen glanced up, biting her bottom lip. "How wild is too wild?"

Cass dragged a superficially reluctant Gwen out of the office to yet another round of cheers. As they waited for the elevator, Cass rattled their joined wrists. "How wild is too wild?" She waggled her eyebrows. "Fifty bucks says we find out tonight."

ERIC REEVES WALKED through the office, navigating cubicles, stopping here and there to exchange a word of encouragement or thanks, sometimes a laugh, with his employees. Sovereign Developments, the real estate development firm he'd founded on dollar bills and a dream, was on the cusp of a huge deal. After securing the rights to develop the Chok Resort on Lake Washington in a battle with David Jameson, an established developer, that had, at times, been brutal, they were waiting for the EPA to approve the environmental engineer's plan. More importantly, they were waiting for the board to agree to *fund* the plan. In the meantime, he'd had to forgo his salary to make sure Sovereign could pay its bills, and he was working a second job to pay his *own* bills.

When the contracts between the parties were signed and Sovereign was officially the development firm of record, Eric would breathe again. Until then, he had a metric crapload of work to do, not the least of which involved long hours at his second job.

"Hey." Eric's assistant, Gretchen, fell into step beside him. "You're on your fifth lap around the office. What's up?"

"I'm not making laps. I'm managing," he answered, smiling absently as he watched an engineer manipulate a drawing on his computer.

"Managing, huh?" She held out a clipboard with several papers attached. "Well, I need you to manage this while you wear the soles off your shoes."

He took the clipboard and scanned the forms. *Payroll. Shit.* "How deep are we in it this time?" Gretchen's studiously blank face was answer enough, but Eric wanted to hear it before he saw the numbers. "Prepare me, Gretch."

"Let's just say we're going to be pushing the limits of our line of credit this pay period."

His stomach tightened as bile rose in his throat. *Still,* he nodded and let one corner of his mouth curl up in a half smile. "Once we're officially cleared on the Chok Resort, you'll be able to stop hovering over the line of credit like a financial mother hen over her little brood of dollar signs."

"I don't hover," Gretchen huffed. Her lips twitched. "Much."

"Right. And I'm actually a leprechaun."

"You're too tall."

He glanced over and arched a brow as he crossed his arms over his chest. His suit pulled at his shoulders. "Are you disparaging my people because I'm a physical anomaly?"

Gretchen laughed out loud, drawing several glances from around the room. "Eric says he's a leprechaun," she announced.

"Where's my pot of gold?" someone shouted.

A discussion ensued regarding leprechauns and what people would do with the gold if they had it. Eric signed forms, keeping one eye on the clipboard and one ear on the chatter. The underlying energy in the room hummed along his skin like a small electrical current. He fed on it. It kept him moving forward, kept him focused and encouraged. As the owner and CEO of Sovereign, he had to ensure the company's financial security and longevity, and there was nothing he wouldn't do to make sure that future was as secure as it could be.

Handing the signed forms to Gretchen with a word of thanks, he shoved his hands in his pockets and headed for the chief financial officer's office.

Dan had been a financial whiz and good friend in college. Eric had recruited him fourteen months ago, spending a pretty penny to make sure Dan came on board. The guy could nearly project markets, could wring out the last cent from every investment and generally make a dollar go further than anyone else Eric knew. Beside himself.

Dan sat behind a beat-up desk, hammering away at his computer. He looked up as Eric came in and closed the door.

"Payroll. When will we be able to afford it?"

Dan swiveled back and forth, his old office chair groaning in protest as he rocked. "We're pushing the financial envelope, Eric. The line of credit won't support another payroll unless we supplement it with some kind of cash influx. The investors won't come up with the cash until the deal is done, and we still don't have a clear picture of how much Preservations' plan is going to cost. If it's too much, the board is going to balk. I have to have twenty grand just to make this week's payroll, so if they postpone their decision, we're screwed. Bottom line? We need your other source of income." Dan spun a pencil between his fingers. "What is it that you do, anyway?"

Eric leaned against the wall and closed his eyes. "Whatever I have to."

Or, to be more specific, whatever his alter ego, Dalton Chase, headline stripper for Beaux Hommes, had to do.

2

ANXIETY RODE THE hollow of Eric's spine like a roller coaster, climbing to the top of his neck and crashing to his tailbone before climbing again. The club take had been dismal.

As he pulled up in front of the Harbormaster apartment building, he gave himself a mental shake. He still had the private party. *Either get in the game and make this pay off, or come up with another strategy.* The bachelorette party should be in full swing, and happy women were spenders. This was his chance to turn the night around. Reaching behind him, he grabbed his briefcase. The hostess had requested a businessman. Lucky him. It was the closest he ever came to mixing his day job with this one. In truth, it made him uncomfortable. He sold day and night. The only difference was the commodity on the table.

The valet looked over his age-scarred Honda with barely concealed disdain.

Eric's free hand tightened into a fist. "Problem?"

"No." Then the valet took in his tailored suit. "Sir."

He tossed the guy his key and stalked away. *One hour, Eric. Shut your shit down for one hour.*

The apartment lobby was immaculate, with a combination of marble floors and patterned blue carpet. He headed straight for the elevator bank, catching a car as a couple of guys exited. The elevator began its smooth ascension. When the car stopped and the doors opened again, Eric pasted on a smile and adjusted his tie.

Time to find out if luck really is a lady.

The knock at the door sent Cass's heart into her throat. *Oh, crap. Crap, crap, crap. It can't be ten o'clock.* But it was. And that meant the evening's entertainment was here. There was normally something to be said for a man who valued punctuality, but at the moment? It was the last thing Cass wanted. No doubt there were going to be questions from the guests, and she hadn't drunk enough to answer them without blushing. Hell, there might not be enough alcohol in the building to save her face from going up in flames.

Grabbing Gwen's hand, Cass wove through the crowd to the front door.

Gwen tugged on Cass's grip. "What's going on?"

"Someone knocked."

Steeling herself, Cass yanked the door open. And stopped breathing. Completely.

Tall, probably six-three or six-four, with broad shoulders and a narrow waist, the man wore a well-fitted business suit of dark gray with subtle pinstriping, complete with a solid, darker vest. A purple paisley tie and matching pocket square rounded out the look. His dark brown hair was damp and, cut in an executive's cut, needed a trim. One broad hand smoothed his jacket. "Gwen Sivern?" he asked her. His voice was as fluid as hot caramel.

Cass pointed at Gwen. "Her." She swallowed hard. "I'm Cass. Wheeler. Cass Wheeler."

A dark, seductive grin revealed dimples.

She'd never had an opinion on dimples. Suddenly she loved them. Craved them. Thought every man should have them.

Shifting his pale green gaze to Gwen, he held out a hand. "Dalton Chase. I'm here to discuss your prenuptial agreement."

Gwen glanced from him to Cass, who shrugged. "I don't have a prenuptial agreement."

"That's…interesting." Dalton flipped open the lower button on his jacket and slipped one hand in his pocket. He focused on Cass. "May I come in?"

Cass moved aside, inadvertently yanking Gwen with her.

Dalton's eyes slipped to their cuffed wrists. His lips twitched. "I see I got here just in time for the fun."

Dreaded heat flooded Cass's cheeks. "I lost the key," she said on a sigh at the same time Gwen squeaked, "It's not what it looks like, I swear."

He stepped into the foyer, closing the door behind him, grinning. "My lucky night. Considering you're cuffed to her, I'm going to take it as a two-for-one special."

Gwen turned in near slow motion and gaped first at Cass and then at Dalton. "You're a stripper."

Cass darted a glance at Dalton. His smile never faltered, but his face seemed to tighten.

"Cass," Gwen all but shouted as she bounced on the balls of her feet. "Tell me you hired me a stripper."

Dalton chuckled. "Well, Gwen, I'm not here to sell you life insurance." He started through the apartment. "Sounds like the fun's centered in here."

Temporary silence fell over the crowd of women when he walked into the large living room, Cass and Gwen right behind him.

He glanced over his shoulder. "I was told you'd have a stereo."

"I, uh, do." *What is* wrong *with me?* She'd seen attractive men and had even dated a couple of exceptionally gorgeous specimens, but there was something about *this* man that was different. She tipped her head toward the entertainment center. "It's on the shelf below the TV."

"Excellent." He nodded toward the women who were watching him with open fascination. "Ladies."

"You're Dalton Chase," breathed one of Gwen's distant cousins whose name Cass couldn't remember.

He smiled at her. "I am."

"Please, Lord, tell me that man is going to take his clothes off. Someone *please* tell me he's going to *take* his clothes *off,*" Tyra, Cass's assistant, said in a stage whisper.

"Oh, he's going to," the bridesmaid-cousin said, reaching for her purse and digging out her wallet with shaking hands.

Cass tried not to smile and failed as the women scrambled to retrieve their handbags.

She'd gone to extremes to keep the evening's entertainment private, asking the club to go so far as to keep her name off the invoice. Hiring a stripper wasn't really a big deal, but the double standards of behavior for men versus women were alive and well in the business world. And she had to face Sovereign's board of directors next week, a board that was notoriously conservative. Plus, she didn't doubt there would be competitors who would try to use the information to paint her as a young, irresponsible wild child and snag the contract out from under her. Too much work had gone into this project to lose it to some small-minded, misogynistic asshat.

Despite all that, she watched Dalton dig through his

briefcase and couldn't help but admire the chiseled line of his jaw and broad sweep of his shoulders. She'd asked the club to send the best. They'd certainly honored her request.

Dalton crouched before the stereo and plugged in his phone, scrolling through his music to find the song he wanted. He cranked the volume before facing the room. "I need a chair."

Three women scrambled to offer theirs.

He winked at the shyest of the group and took the chair she offered before tracing the pad of one of his fingers down the woman's jaw. "Thanks." He leaned forward and kissed her cheek.

To a woman, the room sucked in its breath and several squirmed in their seats.

The song's bass line started low and built as Dalton slowly slid the chair across the room with exaggerated steps. He stopped and crooked his finger at Gwen, but his eyes were on Cass.

She couldn't look away.

"Both of you. C'mere."

The music began to throb, the base thumping in a sexual cadence. Gwen dragged Cass across the floor.

Dalton settled Gwen in the chair and stood Cass behind her, their cuffed wrists resting on Gwen's shoulder.

Pitbull's voice came across the speakers, followed by Christina Aguilera's. Dalton shrugged out of his jacket. Stepping in close enough to Cass that she could feel the heat radiating off his torso, he held the jacket out by one finger. The lyrics paused. He let the jacket fall.

The room went wild.

His hips worked behind Cass in time to the music, his groin randomly brushing her ass.

She curled her fingers into Gwen's shoulder. This was *not* the way this was supposed to have gone. Gwen was supposed to get a lap dance, a little embarrassing sexual innuendo dropped around her, and the women were supposed to get a show. Cass was *not* supposed to be part of the performance.

"Go with it, Ms. Wheeler," he whispered into her ear.

Her breath caught in her chest. He smelled expensive—rich, dark, spicy—and something in her ignited as he ran a finger down her spine. "Cass."

The music built and broke into a techno dance beat.

He grabbed her hips and ground against her. "Cass it is."

Dalton moved around the chair and straddled Gwen's lap, rolling his torso in an impressive move that made him seem boneless. Pulling his tie loose, he left it around his neck as he flicked first his vest then his shirt open. They landed on the floor beside his jacket. He was tan, smooth-skinned and defined in a way that made Cass hunger to run her hands over his body.

Propping a foot lightly on Gwen's thigh, one side of his mouth curled up in a brutally seductive smile. "Help me with my shoe?"

"I can't," Gwen squeaked.

"Just the laces, baby. I'll do the rest."

Gwen reached a shaking hand toward his shoe.

Cass leaned forward and laid her hand over Gwen's so they undid the laces together.

Dalton grinned, wide and shameless. "A threesome. My favorite."

Cass couldn't blink, could only stare at him. He owned the moment, so compelling and utterly sexual in a way she'd never experienced. Not like this. His absolute confidence fueled her bravery. Before she thought it through, she arched a brow and licked her lips. "Seems you've got another shoe."

"So I do." He moved his other foot up to Gwen's thigh. "Be as thorough as you need to be, ladies."

"It's just a shoe," Gwen said, her chest rising and falling rapidly. "How can a shoe be so damn provocative?"

"You're cuffed to another woman, sweetheart, and you're asking me to explain to you what we could do with the laces?" He kicked the shoe off and knelt in front of Gwen, running his hands up the outside of her legs, ankles to hips. With an exaggerated sigh, he placed a hand over his heart. "I only have one night, darling, but for you? I'll do my best to teach you everything I know."

He surged to his feet, hips rolling and thrusting in time to the music. The way he moved had to be illegal in twenty-seven states. Maybe twenty-eight. Or forty. Then he ran his hands over his body.

Cass's nipples pearled. Glancing up, she was stunned to find him watching her.

Eyes brimming with something primitive and dark, he never looked away from Cass as he grabbed Gwen's hand and guided her through removing his belt. He stalked around them. One wide hand moved around Cass's waist to feed the belt across her lower hips. Dalton gripped each end and leaned back, forcing Cass to arch her spine and present her ass. Dropping the belt, he grabbed her hips and moved against her in a smooth pantomime of sex.

Her mind went totally blank. The only thing she could manage was conjuring images of Dalton naked, in bed, pulling some of the same moves. Cass closed her eyes. Her first inclination was to regain control of the moment, to not let anyone—*him*—rule her in the moment.

You've earned a little fun. Screw the moment! her sub-conscious shouted.

Gwen's earlier admonishment to let her hair down suddenly became the best advice ever.

3

ERIC HAD EXPERIENCED a moment of absolute, unanticipated desire when the hostess opened the front door. He'd seen lots of beautiful women, but Cass was something else. At somewhere near six feet in heels, she'd looked up at him with denim-blue eyes framed by long black lashes. Pale pink lips had parted as she'd sucked in a breath. Color had stolen across high cheekbones, and she'd dropped her gaze.

Something inside him had shifted then. Hard. His synapses fired and then spontaneously combusted. He wasn't entirely sure what he'd said, only that he'd made it to the living room without giving in to the impulse to kiss her.

In a strange way, it had made the rest of the night's decisions easier. He'd dance only for her. It wasn't about the money; they were just two people responding to each other. And it had been a damn long time since he'd felt like his body was more than a commodity.

As he tightened the belt, she looked over her shoulder and gave him a slow, sexy smile, rolling her bottom lip under her front teeth and waggling her eyebrows.

Lust flooded his groin.

He ran a hand up her spine and wound his fingers through her dark hair, pulling her head back. *Game. On.*

Her dark blue eyes flared for one brief second.

Eric pulled her toward him. Sliding his palm over her taut abdomen, he swiveled his hips and reveled at the catch of her breath.

Movement caught his attention. Gwen was staring over her shoulder curiously. *Damn it.* He'd gotten so wrapped up in Cass that he'd forgotten the bride. He let the tall, sultry brunette go and shifted his attention to the blonde.

The music bled from Pitbull to the Black Eyed Peas' "Boom Boom Pow."

After dancing with Cass, his cock was threatening to put on a *real* show, but the idea was enough to tone things down.

Stalking around Gwen, he unbuttoned his pants and teased his zipper down.

He made the removal of his pants a seduction, though it wasn't for the benefit of the woman seated in front of him. Inch after inch of skin was revealed until he let them fall away, finally stepping free. Straddling Gwen again, he fought to keep his gaze on her and not the woman cuffed to her. Her free hand was fisted at her waist. Eric picked it up and dragged it down his chest, imagining how Cass's fingers would feel on his heated skin.

Gwen looked up at him, eyes sparkling. "Do that thing with your abs."

He rolled his torso, shoulders to hips.

She screamed and laughed again.

The women in the room went wild.

Eric beckoned the shy one who'd given him her chair. "C'mon, baby girl. Let me thank you appropriately."

She shook her head.

"Go get her," Cass murmured.

Surprised, he glanced at her.

"She's my assistant. Her husband recently left her." True concern colored Cass's eyes. "It would make her feel good."

With a quick nod, he worked his way to the quiet woman. She refused to look up as he danced. Fair. But it didn't work for him. So he pulled her out of her chair and let her stumble into him, saving herself by planting her hands on his chest. He pressed her hands there and encouraged her to touch. That wasn't part of his typical act, but at the moment, it didn't matter.

Moving around the woman, he whispered soft encouragement. When her hand snaked out to put a five in his G-string, he rewarded her with a little extra attention and a second kiss to the cheek. Then he slipped to his briefcase and retrieved a pair of handcuffs and a tiny key. He held both up to the ladies. "Who thinks we should make Gwen work for the key?"

The bride shook her head. "Cass needs to earn it. She's the one who lost the key to start with."

"Is that fair?" he asked the room in general. It was certainly the arrangement he preferred.

The response was unanimous.

"Cass," he murmured. "I'm going to let Gwen go. You'll stay here and earn the key for both of you."

Her eyes sparked and color flooded her cheeks, but she nodded.

"Here's what we're going to do, ladies. I'm going to switch the music to something a little more…appropriate. While my back is turned—" shouts and comments "—you're going to hide money all over Cass. I'm going to find it. I only get to keep what I find." He paused and looked at Cass. "Please, be creative. Very, very creative."

He went to the stereo, smiling at the excited teasing going on behind him. Pushing through the custom mix, he stopped on his favorite song. An electric guitar struck a chord. The bass line fell in behind, and the vocalist slipped into the mix. Highly suggestive lyrics made his blood run hot. Not as hot as the woman who had moved to sit in the center of the room, though. She was spectacular.

She also seemed a little uncomfortable.

Moving around her with slow deliberation, he trailed his fingertips over her bare skin.

She shivered.

He started by plucking bills from the easy-to-reach places and tucked them into his G-string. And bless those women. They'd taken his instructions to heart, tucking bills all over her. He was pretty sure he could now give a good approximation of Cass's measurements. Damn if he wasn't enjoying himself

He dragged the back of his fingers up her arm and under her long hair, wrapping his hand around her neck. Bending close, he locked his gaze with hers. "Did they hide anything in here?"

"You expect me to help you cheat?"

The way she stared at him with undiluted curiosity and open desire made his fingers curl into her neck muscles. His groin tightened.

Gwen and her cheering section were shouting, encouraging him to move on. Dragging his fingers down, over her collarbone and stopping at the glimpse of cleavage his position afforded, he sent her a searching look.

She shrugged, the movement jerky. "You've got to make a living."

Guilt speared through him, shame hot on its heels. This wasn't who he was. He wasn't a user, a seducer for personal purpose or private payout. His fingers hovered over her chest.

"Have mercy on me," she said, blinking up at him with exaggeratedly wide eyes. "Finish your search-and-recover mission so I can go stick my head in the freezer."

"Hot?"

She rolled her shoulders. "I keep telling myself this is your job, but there's still the matter of your fingers on my skin, you know?"

He squashed the urge to stroke her hair. She was right. This, all of this, was about making a living—so why did it feel different? "True enough." Finger-walking his way into her cleavage, he pulled out a twenty. He doubted she'd gotten into the act and tucked the money away herself, particularly between her breasts. "Whom do I thank for their generosity?"

As if she'd read his mind, she winced. "Gwen's payback for me losing the key."

He laughed. "I like Gwen."

She scowled up at him, her heart clearly not in it. "I wasn't supposed to be part of the show."

"Roll with it, baby. It's all in good fun." He gently chucked her under the chin before facing the room, needing a little distance. "Unless you ladies are more dirty-minded than I am, and I seriously doubt that, I've found all the prizes. I'd trade a kiss for a bottle of water."

Several women scrambled for the wet bar.

"Just one," he called after them. On a deep breath, he faced Cass and held up the key. "You were a great sport."

She shrugged. "It wasn't exactly a hardship."

Heat burned his cheeks, and he was both embarrassed and charmed by his reaction. The shy woman from the group was the first to make it back to him with a bottle of water, and he accepted it, this time brushing a soft kiss over her lips. "Thanks, beautiful."

A strange expression passed over Cass's face, one that said Eric had just done something profound. Hell if he knew what it was beyond kindness. Then Cass was gone, making excuses about checking on food and drinks, ensuring guest comfort and anything else she could toss out in a rush.

He watched her move through the crowd, absently rubbing her cuff-free wrist. Gwen bounded over to her and the two exchanged a few words and a quick hug before the bride became the center of attention once again. Gwen shot him bright-eyed looks when she thought he wasn't paying attention, and those looks unnerved him. Clearly, Gwen was up to something. For all that the woman feigned innocence, he'd bet the entire evening's take she had a devious streak.

Grabbing a pair of Elmo sleep pants from his briefcase, he slipped into them and padded around the room, flirting, picking up empty glasses and refilling others.

"You don't have to do that."

He glanced over his shoulder to find Cass closing in on him. "What? Pick up?"

"That, and serve."

"Habit." He shrugged. "I've got another half an hour before my time's up. I can dance if you'd prefer." And didn't that offer have to claw its way out of his chest? He wanted her to see him as more than a stripper, wanted to tell her he was busting his ass to be more than this, but the words wouldn't come.

She shrugged. "It's cool. Just realize I don't expect you to do anything like that."

"You hired me."

The discomfort on her face made him want to apologize. In fact, he started to, but she interrupted. "You're right. I just feel a little awkward treating you like..." She stared at her feet as she chewed on her bottom lip.

"Like a side of delectable beef?"

She huffed out a breath. "I suppose."

The familiar white lie slipped out before he could stop himself. "I'm okay with this, Cass. If I wasn't, I couldn't do what I do."

Gwen bounded up, beer in hand. "I want to go to Cinderblock and dance." She glanced between them and smiled. "They're open until two, so we've got a couple of hours to get our groove on."

"Sure," Cass answered absently, shifting her attention to Gwen. "We can wrap up here and be at the club in under thirty."

The bride shifted innocent eyes on him. "Want to come, Dalton?"

He opened his mouth to politely decline.

Gwen interrupted. "Don't say no. Please?"

"Cass?" Asking her seemed right, because if he went, he'd be off the clock and on his own, and this time he was going to dance *with* her, not *for* her. He would touch her body. And chances were good he'd stop thinking altogether and simply let things go where they would. "Would you be comfortable with me tagging along?"

She looked at him, those blue eyes nearly bottomless. "I'd love to have you..." Her breath caught and her eyes widened. "Join us! I'd love to have you join us."

The strange connection he'd felt earlier sparked, an electric live wire running between them. He didn't, *couldn't,* drag his eyes away when he answered. "Give me an extra half hour to run home and grab some decent clubbing clothes. They're not a tie-required kind of place, but I'm pretty sure pants aren't optional."

Cass's mouth opened and closed a couple of times, yet nothing came out.

Gwen slipped an arm around her waist and addressed Eric. "See you there."

And that, as the saying went, was that.

CASS MOVED ON AUTOPILOT as she rounded up the large party, gave them the address for the club and made sure everyone with keys was sober. As the last of the women left the apartment, Cass raced to her closet, grabbed her favorite little black dress and slipped it on. She swiped on some extra mascara and dabbed on perfume. Then she pulled out the man-killing red lipstick. It was her favorite accessory when she wanted to feel powerful, but she rarely wore it. More often than not it suited her just fine to be part of the scenery rather than the focal point. Not that she was a wallflower. Far from it. She just got so tired of men passing judgment based on her appearance and totally discounting her brain. Lipstick poised at her lips, she hesitated.

"What are you doing?" she asked her reflection. "Nothing can happen between you. You know it. What he is could ruin you."

"You coming, Cass?" Gwen stepped into the master bathroom. "Oh, hey. The red lipstick. My Spidey Sense told me you were into Dalton."

"I just…" She shook her head. "It's so stupid."

"Why?" Gwen moved to stand beside her, slipping an arm around Cass's waist. "How long has it been since you had a little fun? *Serious* fun—the kind that's slightly reckless and totally irresponsible."

Cass studied her best friend's reflection in the mirror as she thought, really thought, about the question. "I don't remember." The answer depressed her. She closed her eyes and sagged against the counter.

"That's what I figured," Gwen said on barely a whisper. "You've turned into the person we swore we'd never become, the one who loses her life to the job, becomes the job, is only the job." Reaching up, she gently unpinned Cass's hair and ran her fingers through the unruly waves as the mass tumbled free. "Live a little. Dance with Dalton tonight."

"He's a stripper."

"You could've been a stripper."

Cass's eyes flashed open. "What?" she choked.

"You're gorgeous. It's one of the things you hide behind, using your looks like a shield to keep people at bay." Gwen rubbed her arm briskly. "It's one of the reasons you have your nickname."

"I'm *not* an Ice Princess." The words were hard, but damn it, she hated being called frigid.

"Prove it." Gwen squeezed Cass's hand then let go, staring at their side-by-side reflections. "Bring the lipstick or don't, but we're going."

"He's not going to show up."

Gwen snorted and shook her head. "We talked about this, Negative Nancy."

"Let me change—"

"No."

The single word was hard and uncompromising. Cass looked up, surprise pushing her eyebrows up her forehead. "No?"

"You put on what made you feel pretty, seductive and desirable. It stays. Let's go." Gwen spun and started out of the bathroom.

Cass pushed off the vanity and raced past Gwen. "I'll hurry!" She grabbed skinny jeans and a short white top.

Stripping quickly, she pulled the shirt on and hopped on first one leg and then the other as she worked herself into the jeans. She shoved her feet into the first pair of stilettos she could reach. "Ready," she shouted.

"Lipstick?"

Cass paused and gazed at the tube she'd tossed on her bed. "What the hell," she muttered before calling out to Gwen, "I'll put it on in the car."

Grabbing the lipstick, she stalked from the room, a little extra sway to her hips.

THE CLUB WASN'T QUITE as crowded as normal, probably due to the weather. That was fine with Cass. It meant she had more room to move. Gwen had been right. Dancing was exactly what Cass had needed.

Five or six songs into the evening, she finally stopped watching the door for Dalton. Disappointment that he hadn't shown proved a bitter pill.

Gwen had hit her where it hurt when she'd pointed out Cass was turning into the person they'd sworn to each other they'd never become. Becoming that woman, the one who was so focused on her career she forgot how to live, terrified her. It made her that much more of her father's daughter, and that was a connection she wanted to sever regardless of the cost. She'd admittedly swung the emotional pendulum toward the opposite extreme when she'd decided to hit on Dalton, but it would have been fun.

Weaving through the crowd, she reached the bar without much hassle.

The bartender, an attractive guy with obvious Nordic heritage, leaned toward her. "What can I get you, beautiful?"

"Michelob Light in the bottle."

"A simple beer girl. You may have just stolen my heart."

"Simple? Never. Stolen your heart?" Cass shrugged with easy nonchalance. "Like a thief in the night, baby."

The bartender slid the beer across the deep bar. "On the house for the thief, then."

Several bills landed beside the beer. "I've got her covered."

Cass rolled her eyes and started to tell the stranger to shop somewhere else, but he leaned in and his breath whispered hot through her hair. "Sorry I'm late."

Her heart stuttered before picking up a hard, tattooing rhythm. Lifting her beer and taking a long draw, she was half amused and half irritated to find that her hand was shaking.

The bartender watched them, clearly assessing the man at her back. "I'm under the impression the lady doesn't need someone to buy her drinks."

"It's not a matter of need, buddy. Tonight's all about want. But if she doesn't want me to buy her a drink, I trust she'll say so."

The physical presence behind her retreated a step.

"I appreciate the generosity," she interjected, moving into that hard, hot body and pressing against him.

The bartender shrugged and moved on to the next order with an easy smile.

Turning, she looked up into stormy green eyes. "Thanks."

"You seem to have a champion." Dalton's tone was cool. "You know him?"

"Nope. I imagine he's just being courteous." She took another sip of her beer. "You want something to drink?"

Dalton wrapped his hand around hers and lifted the bottle to his lips, taking a long, slow draw.

She couldn't help but stare at the way his throat worked as he swallowed. Images of his head thrown back, lips parted, shoulders bunched, the muscles and tendons in his neck straining flashed like Polaroid shots, each drifting to the floor of her mind to lie in a suggestive pile. Desire-fueled embarrassment burned up the back of her neck as she mentally undressed him where he stood.

"Dalton!" Gwen wiggled her way to his side and slid an arm around his waist.

He casually draped an arm over her shoulder and released Cass's beer. "And how's my favorite bride tonight?"

Said bride preened a little. "Better, now that you're here. We're under full-frontal attack from the natives."

"Hmm. I'm more a rear-approach kind of guy."

Cass choked on her beer. Ignoring Gwen's waggling eyebrows, she wheezed and gasped, eyes watering.

Gwen absently waved a hand in her direction. "Don't pay any attention to her. She likes sex but has to warm up before she gives good innuendo."

Her mouth fell open. "Warm... I don't... Up..."

Gwen tipped her chin to bat her eyes at Dalton. "Want to dance?"

Tapping the tip of her nose, he gave a single nod. "That's what I came for."

Sharp irritation cut through Cass as the two wordlessly abandoned her for the dance floor. What the hell was wrong with her? She was normally so smooth and in control of situations involving men, situations like *this*. She'd teased and flirted with the bartender without thinking about it. With Dalton? She was one short step from needing behavioral anti-seizure medication. Embarrassed, she stewed a bit and watched her best friend and...whatever he was get their groove on.

They moved together so easily, Dalton complementing Gwen's every twist and turn. His hands slid over her in a casually suggestive manner. She followed his direction. They were good together, and Cass found herself scowling. An uncomfortable sensation she was entirely unwilling to consider burned behind her belly button. Wrapping her free arm around her waist, she fisted the hem of her shirt and continued to sip her drink as she fought to ignore what she feared was jealousy. She was *not* jealous.

"You're looking a little fierce, beautiful."

She glanced toward the owner of the voice.

The bartender stood behind her, a towel thrown over his shoulder.

Her attention drifted back to the dance floor, and she rolled her head from side to side. "The night isn't going the way I planned."

"It goes against every fiber of my being, but if you want to make him sit up and take notice, I'll help out."

This time she faced him. "Every fiber of your being, huh?"

"Pretty much, yeah." Hands on his hips, he dropped his chin to his chest and closed his eyes. Then he took a deep breath and focused his light blue gaze on her. "Let's go." He tossed his towel on the bar, grabbed her hand and hauled her toward the dance floor. Waving at the DJ booth, he gave a signal and received a nod in return. "My name's Todd, and you're going to owe me a drink."

"I'm Cass. And if dancing with me is that much of a hardship, why do it?"

"After seeing how you moved earlier? Dancing with you is no hardship at all. I just have a feeling that not taking you home is going to be one of my life's greatest regrets."

She arched a brow. "You seem certain I'd go home with

you. I don't know whether to admire your self-confidence or suggest you kiss my ass."

His mouth feathered up at one corner. "I'd settle for your admiration."

Cass laughed. "I believe I'm rather fond of you, Todd."

The song wound down and the DJ's voice, deep and suggestive, came across the sound system. "This one is designed to help you ladies get under his skin."

Music poured out of speakers, the electric tempo fast. Every solitary bass note pounded through her core and settled between her thighs.

Todd lifted her arms over her head. Her shirt slipped up, and he traced his fingertips down her bare sides. Hands at her waist, he encouraged her to turn away from him. "Listen to the lyrics and do whatever feels right."

She closed her eyes and began to move, following the soft suggestions of his hands, letting him mold his body to hers. The drumbeat fell into the song. At the same time, the lyrics registered—lyrics that promised uncomplicated, no-strings-attached sex. Her irritation morphed to sensual hunger as everything in her tuned in to the seduction of the music.

4

ERIC SUSPECTED HE'D irritated Cass when he led Gwen to the dance floor. Part of him reveled in the snap of energy between them while the other part warned him he was fueling a flame he had no hope of controlling. She wouldn't dial it back because he told her to. Granted, he'd just met her, but a large part of his job was reading women, and he was good at it.

He also knew himself, knew he was skating the fine line between casual flirtation and dangerous intent, and, for the first time, he wasn't sure which side of the line he should come down on.

"I get the impression your body's here—" Gwen rested a hand between his pecs "—but your mind's dancing with someone else."

He automatically smiled charmingly. "I'm good."

"Oh, you're the best."

"What's with that look?" Spinning her, he settled her back to his chest so he didn't have to see the almost sympathetic compassion in her eyes.

"You're attracted to Cass but you're pulling the same bullshit maneuvers she always has to deal with. I had higher hopes for you."

Eric froze. "Excuse me?"

"Don't get all bent." She kept dancing as she spoke. "You're blindly poking a stick through cage bars, not sure whether you'll tag a lion or a lamb."

He started to move again, slower now. "Which is she?"

"That's for you to figure out, handsome." She faced him, her gaze fierce. "Just don't be stupid about it. Now, go dance with Cass."

He found himself smiling at the pissed-off pixie staring up at him. She had no problem putting him in his place. He respected that. Chances were good Cass would be the same way, and the thought made his blood run hotter. Leaning in, he placed a soft kiss against Gwen's forehead.

"You're a little scary for such a wisp of a woman."

"I come from a long line of terrifying wisps." She glanced around him and grinned at whatever she saw. "Wow. That's hot."

Eric didn't want to know what had Gwen smiling manically, yet he couldn't help but look. What he saw lit him up brighter than holiday fireworks.

Other dancers had given the pair a little extra space, watching as they moved against each other in a sensual feast of touching and caressing. Lips parted, Cass made love to the music. The bartender's hands traced over her body, brushing the soft curves of her hips. A faint smile teased her lips when he bent low and whispered in her ear, but her eyes remained on Eric's.

Eric didn't recall starting toward the couple. All he knew was that he was halfway to them when Gwen grabbed his hand and stepped ahead of him so it appeared she was pulling him across the floor.

"I want to switch," she called out to Cass over the music.

Cass moved her eyes away from him with slow deliberation. "You got first pick."

"Doesn't matter. I'm the bride, and I want to switch."

Cass frowned. "That excuse is getting old."

"Maybe, but it doesn't make it any less true." She slipped in between the bartender and Cass. "Hi. I don't need your name. I'm just going to call you Captain Morgan, 'kay?"

He slid right into the music again, watching her with clear amusement. "You can call me whatever you want."

Eric reached out and caught Cass's hand as she started toward the ladies' table. "Hey. Song's not over."

She stopped and glanced at Eric, her eyes neutral despite the high color riding her cheeks. "I got the impression your dance partner ditched you for the King of Rum over there."

Yep, she was irritated. He shrugged. "I get thrown over at the end of every set for the next guy to hit the stage, so I'm used to it."

"You're not really going to use that line, are you?"

Narrowing his eyes, he reached for her hand. "C'mon, Cass. I want to dance with you."

"Would it kill you to ask?"

"Might." It was fast becoming clear he'd missed the lamb and hit the lion as he pulled her through the throng of gyrating bodies.

Without warning, he spun her and, chest to her back, ran a hand up her stomach, between her breasts and over her shoulder. He snugged her tight to his chest. Her breath hitched, the little gasp shivering through his arm. His heartbeat did this funny freeze-then-run-away thing. He drew a shallow breath to say something—who knew what?—and instead got a whiff of her perfume, subtle, lush, erotic. It delivered a punch of arousal straight to his groin.

Cass wiggled.

He didn't let go. Instead, he pulled her hair aside with his free hand and laid his lips against the shell of her ear. "What are you wearing?"

"Clothes. Now let me go."

The music wound down, but he didn't move.

She struggled.

He tightened his hold.

"Let. Me. Go." Every world was issued on the threat of implied retaliation.

"Dance with me, Cass." Moving against her, he whispered, "Just dance."

She stood still long enough he was sure she was going to turn him down.

His stomach tightened. *Nerves? No way. No damn way.*

Then she leaned into him and, hooking her arms around his neck, began to sway to the music. "One song." Subdued at first, her hips gradually took up a more insistent, primal rhythm. Fingernails raked the skin of his neck and wove into his nape.

Goose bumps scattered across his arms.

Cass was a siren, moving beneath the colored lights and through the artificial smoke that wafted across the dance floor as if she belonged there. Men watched her. Women mimicked her. Eric wanted her. Craved her. Ached for her.

Intense hunger burned through him, a flash fire of desire that incinerated his reserve of common sense. He tightened his hold on her and let their bodies twist and turn and stroke and touch in an elemental way that fed his desire, intensified the building ache in his cock and transformed preliminary want into undeniable need.

He'd clearly come down on one side of the imaginary line he'd drawn—the side of seduction. Whether it was his or hers remained to be seen.

Regardless, it was only one night. Tomorrow he'd go back to the problems of Eric Reeves.

CASS'S PULSE THUNDERED as the song faded and a new one rolled across the crowd, this one more heavy metal than heavy petting.

Dalton's hand settled on her lower back, hot as a brand. Slight pressure steered her across the room and toward the small hallway leading to the restrooms. The hallway was lit. The area outside it wasn't.

Dalton curled his fingers over the low-slung waistband of her jeans. His fingers brushed over the silk of her skin and the satin of her thong, paused, and then fisted the denim roughly enough to make her gasp.

Equal parts desire and sexual fervor rushed through her head in a whitewash of noise.

With a small tug, he spun her around and closed in, pressing her back against a wall in the darkest corner. The smell of his soap, earthy and masculine, washed over her. Her lips parted.

He dipped his head slowly, giving her ample time to protest his obvious intent. When she offered none, he claimed her mouth. No games. No pretense. No hesitation.

She gripped his shoulders and met his hunger touch for touch, taste for taste.

His tongue flicked over hers. The pad of one thumb traced her chin even as the rest of his hand cupped her neck. Long fingers of his free hand wrapped around the back of her head and cradled the shallow dip at the top of her spine. Encouraging her forward, he pulled her up and deeper into the kiss. He nibbled her bottom lip before gently suckling the same.

The faint taste of hops hovered on the tip of his tongue. She yielded to him on an exhale.

He owned her mouth, directed her body and became her anchor in a brewing emotional storm. Long-forgotten desire curled through her pelvis, warm and wanting. One kiss barely begun, and already she wanted more.

His fingertips traced the hollow of her spine, lower and lower until they slipped over her ass and hauled her forward to straddle his thigh.

Cass gasped, the sound acting like a starting gun to the man who had held her so carefully. He was suddenly everywhere. The kiss that had been gentle, tentative even, morphed into something fierce, demanding, dominating. Dalton simply possessed her. He tilted her head a fraction to better accommodate the slant of his mouth. His lips moved with ruthless precision, driving her higher and wringing a sound of pure desperation from her, a sound he swallowed with a groan.

She fought to give as well as she got. Her arms went around his neck at the same time she wrapped a leg around his hips. He gripped her knee and encouraged her higher. The heavy ridge of his erection rode the seam of her sex and ripped from her throat an erotic whimper laced with need. She rocked against him, meeting his small thrusts.

Someone coughed as they walked by.

Cass whipped her chin away, turning her face into the corner. *What the hell was she doing?* There was a huge difference between letting her hair down and getting it on in public. Her father would declare this the ultimate weakness, right behind love, and would humiliate her for it endlessly. Time to scale things down and regroup. She'd reclaim her raging hormones and shove them back into their box.

That was the problem, though. Those hormones? They didn't want to be put away. No, they wanted to stay out and play with Dalton.

"Cass?" His voice, deep and gravelly with undisguised want, scraped over her. Clearing his throat, he lowered her leg but didn't move away from her.

"What is this?" she asked softly.

"This?"

"Whatever's happening between us. One minute we're dancing and the next—" she waggled a hand between them "—this."

He leaned back a bit to watch her through hooded eyes, framing her upper body when he propped his arms against the wall on each side of her. His lower body pinned her. All around them, people danced and talked and drank and lived without paying them much attention. When he finally answered, his words stole her breath. "I hope *this* is more than a single dance but less than a heartache."

She nodded. They were so on the same page. It could be one night, a night no one would, or could, know about. Anything else could ruin her reputation and get her fired from the Sovereign project. She lifted her chin, determined. "Tonight, then."

The air between them became a charged milieu, electric and volatile, as they stared at each other.

He moved in so close his lips brushed hers when he asked, "Want to get out of here?"

"It's Gwen's bachelorette party. I can't just leave." But she wanted to. Badly.

"I understand." Glancing at his watch, the slight tension around his eyes eased. "Bar closes in thirty minutes." Full lips tipped up and green eyes glinted in the low light. "We could just occupy this corner until then."

Caught between the desire to do just that and a potential panic attack at doing just that, she settled her hands on his hips and gently pushed. "Believe it or not, I'm not entirely comfortable with public displays."

"You dance like a hedonist yet you're worried about being caught kissing me?" There was an underlying edge to the words.

She tipped her chin up and met his cooling stare. "I'm a relatively private person. I dance, yes, but that's entirely different from being caught in a dark corner with someone's hands down my pants."

He closed his eyes for a second and took a deep breath before nodding. "Okay. I respect that." He stepped away, creating space between them she didn't want. "You want to kill the time on the dance floor?"

"Why don't we find Gwen? Once she leaves, we can, too," she answered, scanning the club for her friend.

"Sure." He took her hand and laced their fingers together.

She didn't comment, but let him lead her through the crowd toward the table they'd held. Several of the women from the party were there. They looked over at her and Dalton, taking in their linked hands. A couple of suggestive glances were exchanged.

Cass stepped forward, but Dalton tightened his grip. "You ladies know where our lovely little bride has run off to?"

"Last we heard, she was going to dance with the bartender one more time before she headed home. Said she missed Dave."

He smiled. "Ladies," Dalton said abruptly. "Have a nice evening."

Squashing the urge to squirm, she slipped her arm around Dalton's waist.

He relaxed his grip on her only slightly.

The music cued up, and the mass of people on the dance floor began to move.

Dalton bent low. "Your car or mine?"

5

THE RIDE TO CASS'S apartment passed in silence, giving Eric time to think and, ultimately, feel guilty. He should have told Cass his real name before kissing her. Letting her go on believing he was "Dalton" was far too close to lying by omission. Still, there was simply too much to risk by sharing his real name with a near stranger. If things went south between them, it would be a simple thing for her to out him in conversations with her business associates and friends, women who came to the club who could tie CEO Eric Reeves to stripper Dalton Chase. And if the ultraconservative investors in his company found out, he could lose everything. He couldn't move forward without their money. Period. And if he couldn't move forward, he was sliding down progress's steep slope. There was no standing still in this business. So, no. He wouldn't tell Cass his real name.

At the same time, he wasn't giving up this night with her. He wanted it, wanted her, too much, in a way he'd never felt before. The fire she'd ignited in him now threatened to incinerate him. He had to experience her. She'd made it clear they had tonight and tonight only. Eric wasn't foolish enough to believe that would be enough, and the thought of living with only that limited taste of her already chaffed. But he agreed—one night was all they could risk.

Needing a distraction, he reached for the radio at the same moment Cass did. Their hands brushed over one another, the simple contact stopping Eric's breath. It took a moment to realize she'd frozen, too.

"What do you want to listen to?" He couldn't look at her when he asked the question.

"It's preset to one-oh-seven-point-one."

"You like hard rock?" Surprise infused his every word.

"What, you assumed I was a Top 40 girl?"

He laughed. "I guess."

"Shame on you." She took the Broadway exit.

A deep guitar riff ripped through the car.

Eric leaned back in his seat. Their shared music preference fueled Eric's curiosity, made him want to know more about her. It was a bad idea, digging into what made her tick, and he was well aware of it. That kind of knowledge would add a very personal layer to tonight's pleasure. It didn't stop him, though.

He reached forward and turned the radio down. "Tell me something about yourself."

Absently tucking her hair behind one ear, she stole a quick glance in his direction. "What do you want to know?"

Everything. "Anything."

"I'm the oldest child."

"How many siblings?"

"I have one younger brother."

Shifting onto his hip to face her, one corner of his mouth lifted. "Me, too. Sucks being the oldest."

Her shoulders hunched forward, and he ached to

soothe her, to say he understood. Then she seemed to catch herself and sat up. Her death grip on the steering wheel belied her calm exterior. "Yeah." She softly cleared her throat. "Yeah, it does."

"What does your brother do?"

She glanced at him, meeting his eyes this time. "Everything right."

Muscles along his spine tightened. "Which leaves you doing everything wrong."

She snorted delicately. "Pretty much. Now your turn."

His hesitation stalled the conversation for a moment before he finally gathered the nerve to reveal a piece of himself. "I'm the oldest, too. My parents were killed in an accident with a logging truck several years ago. I basically raised my little brother."

She didn't say anything, just stared ahead as she drove.

Her silence made him want to scream. Instead, he rambled on.

"Blake was just a kid, really. He struggled, got a little out of control—violent in school, destructive out of school. I was shoved into the role of parent and provider with no clue how to be either. Not really. I was trying to go to college, but corralling him took most of my energy." He paused, not quite willing to explain how losing his parents had wrecked him yet raising Blake had left him no real time to grieve. Focusing on Blake's struggles was easier, and he felt the need to justify the primary choice he'd made to provide for Blake. "Stripping was fast money I desperately needed."

"What did you do with Blake at night?"

"At first I hired someone to stay with him, but that was a total fail. Eventually I made friends with some of the other dancers and they'd volunteer to stay with him while I worked. The strong male presence kept him in the house and off the streets."

"But why do you continue to strip?"

"To put Blake through college and pay the bills." No need to explain "the bills" weren't just his but those of his company, as well. Anxiety rose as he remembered the financial predicament he was in. "It's been a nightmare of epic proportions, keeping the bills paid and him in school."

A hard blush stole over his cheeks and his breath caught. *What the hell was that? Super sexy, telling your one-night stand you're broke, Reeves.* "I'm sorry. I—"

"Don't apologize for telling the truth," she said, pulling into a parking lot behind a tall apartment building. "I've had plenty of SpaghettiOs nights myself." She stared straight ahead as she shut off the engine.

He'd had one-night stands before. More than he cared to admit, actually. But he'd never been seriously interested in the woman, not like he was with Cass. She was clever and strong and spirited, yet still reserved and cautious. She reminded him of a ten-thousand-piece, three-dimensional puzzle. It would take a lifetime to get all the pieces together to form the true picture of who she was and what made her tick. But he only had until sunrise.

Leaning in, he threaded his fingers through her hair and pulled her close. She tasted like chocolate and woman and sensual promises. She smelled like feminine desire and warmth and peppermint shampoo. She felt like silk and muscle and tightly coiled energy under his work-roughened hands. And he wanted it all. Every last bit of it.

No more hesitating, no more guilt, no more stupid internal monologues with his conscience. He liked her. He craved her. He wanted her more than he'd ever wanted another woman. And he was going to have her.

But it was more than all those things combined. He'd been able to share the tiniest corner of truth with Cass—that raising Blake had been tough—and she hadn't played the sympathy card or asked him a thousand questions. She simply accepted that he'd done what he had to do and had listened and understood. For the first time since his parents' deaths, Eric didn't feel quite so alone.

And he knew one night with Cass simply wouldn't be enough. But it was the perfect place to start.

THE HEAVY ENTRY DOOR to her apartment swung shut with a decisive *whump.* Every hair on Cass's body stood up, aware of Dalton's proximity as he moved behind her. A hot, hard hand closed around the front of her throat. Moving in close, he swept her hair to the side. "Where, Cass?"

"Where what?" The question was so soft she hardly heard her voice over the shallow breaths that scalded her ear.

"Where do you want me to take you the first time?"

The hand at her throat slid down, across her collarbone and over the swell of one breast. He brushed a thumb over her nipple and she arched into his touch. Heat flooded her sex, left her pelvis heavy with wanting.

"Where, Cass? If you don't answer me, it will be right here."

She drew a breath to answer.

"Took too long." He curled one hand around the back of her pants as he reached down with the other and undid her belt. "Lose the shoes, then the jeans."

"The coat—"

"No time."

His hands were there and then gone as he stepped

away. Foil crinkled and tore. She kicked her pants free and, before she could form a coherent thought, he spun her around, his hips pinning her to the wall.

"You need to call a halt now if you're going to. Once we start, I don't know if I can stop." He licked a narrow line up the side of her neck and nipped her jaw. "I want you too damn bad, Cass."

"Don't stop. Please, don't stop." Her plea was half sob, half groan. Overwhelming desperation made her demand to have him just like this, right here.

Bending at the knees, he hooked his arms behind her thighs and lifted.

She gasped, wrapping her arms around his neck.

A quick shift and he was poised at her entrance. "Guide me in, baby."

Reaching between them, she found the head of his cock. Her eyes widened as she maneuvered him into place. "You're freaking huge."

"Discuss my pride later." He thrust forward and groaned. "So damn tight."

Cass stroked his thick length as he worked his way in. His width and girth stretched her to that beautiful convergence of pain and pleasure, filling her impossibly while leaving her squirming to both take more now and make him slow down. She wanted all of him and pulled him deeper in encouragement, an involuntary whimper escaping. Her fingertips finally brushed his testicles when he was seated as far as he could go.

"Lean back."

She clasped her hands around his neck and did as he bade, letting her eyes slip closed.

Chest heaving, he slid nearly out of her and paused. "Cass."

She looked into sea-green eyes and opened her mouth

to respond. That's when he drove back into her. The scream that ripped out of her throat was one of absolute ecstasy. He stretched her just as she'd craved, filled her, made her want it hard and fast and deep. "Again," she cried.

Dalton didn't answer. Instead, he set a brutal pace. Every upstroke raked across her clit. Every withdrawal dragged the top of his erection over the same. The stimulation was fierce and unrelenting. His breath came in hard draws, matching her own. His fingers cupped her ass and curled in, but he never slowed down, furiously pumping into her.

The orgasm ripped through her without warning. Nothing had ever felt like this, as if she was being shattered and made whole, flying and falling, dying and living. All at once. All together. Completely out of control.

His wordless shout accompanied a particularly deep thrust, and she felt his cock pulsing inside her as her walls continued to spasm, his thrusts becoming short and sporadic.

"Dalton!" she shouted as a second, smaller orgasm laid claim to her body. Rocking against him, desperate for friction, he pinned her to the wall with his chest and one arm. He slipped his freed hand between them to rapidly strum her clit.

"Ride it out, baby," he whispered against her lips. "Ride it out."

She seized his mouth with her own, winding her hands through his hair as she rode both his cock and his hand. A harsh moan shook her as the orgasm crested. The rapid manipulation of her body, the way he continued to drive into her with shallow thrusts, made the second orgasm drag on and on. Finally, unable to take any more, she gripped his wrist and squeezed at the same time she tore her mouth away. "Enough."

"Not even close to enough," he said, panting against the side of her neck. "Not even close."

There was no way to stop her legs from buckling when her feet hit the floor.

Dalton caught her, scooped her up and carried her deeper into the apartment. "Bedroom?"

Pointing was a major win because it meant she had at least minor muscle control.

Through the door, he paused. "Nice."

The iron headboard of her queen-size bed bumped the wall as he laid her down. He moved to the foot and tugged the bed away from the wall with a wicked look. "No need for the neighbors to know what we're up to."

"Something tells me they've already figured it out."

"It'll give them something to talk about…or aspire to."

"Yeah, it wasn't bad for a cold start."

He threw back his head and laughed, loud and long. "Not bad, huh? I see the lady has high expectations. Good thing I can deliver."

"Are you always so arrogant?"

"It's only arrogance if you only *think* you're good. I *know* I am, and so do you."

She gave an exaggerated yawn. "Talk, talk, talk."

He moved to her feet. "Hands on the headboard."

Cass propped herself up on her elbows as butterflies maneuvered wildly in her belly. "Why?"

"Hands. On. The headboard."

The iron was cold and rough against her palms as she wound her fingers around the vertical bars. She wanted to ask what he was up to, but she also simply wanted to do what he directed without demanding explanation, to just once not need diagrams and contingency plans for her life. Tonight wasn't meant to be planned out but rather spontaneously experienced. Closing her eyes, she sighed. To experience him meant giving up control of the moment. She sucked at that.

"Stop thinking so hard." He stroked her ankle then up her calf. "Bend your knees, feet flat on the bed. Good girl." A gentle push spread her legs.

Embarrassment scalded her neck and settled across her cheeks. She'd never bared herself to a man before. Not like this. Never so completely. There was a defenselessness to it, a lack of any pretension or place to withdraw to, and the knowledge made her want to clamp her legs together and cover her breasts. It wasn't that she was a prude. She just wasn't experienced in some areas. Allowing herself to be so vulnerable was at the top of that list.

Soft caresses and warm lips started up the inside of her leg.

Every muscle in her body spasmed. If allowing herself to be vulnerable held the top spot for sexual inexperience in her life, oral sex ran a close second. Twice she'd allowed a man to go down on her. Twice she'd wondered what the hell all the fuss was about. Sighing, she tried to relax into the sensations of Dalton's lips and teeth, tongue and breath as he worked his way up her body.

One muscled arm wrapped around her thigh and across her hips. "Easy, Cass."

"I don't know if this is a good idea." She couldn't bring herself to look at him, instead staring at the ceiling.

"When is oral sex ever a *bad* idea?"

"I…" She rolled her bottom lip under her front teeth and worried it. "Always?"

He propped up on one elbow and gazed up her body. "Look at me, baby." When she didn't, he huffed out a

Stripped Down

short breath. "Fine. If you don't want to talk about it, I'll show you why you're wrong."

Smooth, firm lips traveled the line between hip and mons. He nipped the insides of her thighs. Every exhale seemed directed to some sensitive spot designed to drive her mad. When his tongue danced around her clit but didn't touch it, she growled—actually growled.

He settled onto his knees on the floor. "Let go of the headboard." Hooking his arms around her thighs, he slid her down the bed until she hung off the edge. "Vulnerable" reached a new level of discomfort when he propped her feet on his shoulders, his lips roaming over the inside of her ankles.

Dalton never stopped moving—hands on her hips moving to caress her ass, feather-soft kisses along the inside of her thighs, soft words she didn't quite understand, the quickening of his breath. Then he paused, wrapped his hands around her thighs to hold them open and—

Cass's back bowed off the bed when he dragged his tongue up the seam of her sex and over her clit.

He didn't pause, didn't give her a moment to sort out her thoughts. No, he pushed her. His tongue did impossible things, delving deep before flicking over that swollen bundle of nerves that had become her fault line's epicenter.

Her hips bucked wildly. She didn't care. All she wanted was for him to…to… A wild scream built in her throat.

As if she'd spoken aloud, Dalton pushed her legs wider and wrapped his lips around her clit. Then he sucked, rolling and pinching the little bud between his lips and tongue.

The orgasm burned through her like a wind-fueled wildfire over parched grassland. It consumed her and left nothing behind but ash. Still, she was carried away by gust after gust of pleasure that surged through her body. She gripped Dalton's hair and rode his mouth with wanton abandon.

He brought her down slowly, stroking her belly and hips, murmuring nearly unintelligible praise against her sex. She wanted to laugh and cry and plead for him to do it again and never. Every sense was so incredibly hypersensitive. When he began to move away from her, she scooted up the bed and wrapped her arms around her knees. "Leaving?"

A funny look passed over his face, and suddenly he was crawling up the bed, his hard shaft bobbing with his every feline move. Pressing her back into the mattress, he loomed over her. "I'm not quite ready for intermission, thanks."

Neither was she.

6

ERIC OPENED HIS EYES and squinted into the watery sunlight burning through the last of the morning fog. His head lolled to one side. A tumbled mass of loosely curled, light brown hair was spread over half his pillow. The smell of Cass's peppermint shampoo was woven through the pillowcase, and he'd dreamed of her in the couple of hours of sleep he'd stolen.

She'd been amazing last night—willing, eager...surprised. When he'd discovered she truly hadn't ever had a night of passion, he'd silently vowed to become her best memory. It was all he could do since he couldn't be her only. He had put everything he had into being her best. Why it mattered was still lost on him.

Cass rolled toward him, still asleep. The urge to pull her into his arms was so strong he actually reached for her before stopping abruptly when thoughts of his company and his dreams crept into his consciousness. Last night had been about seduction and mutual gratification. Nothing more. Now he needed to get back to business—the Chok Resort and stopping Jameson from finding a way to crowd him out.

Just one small mistake and Eric could lose control of

this deal. That couldn't, *wouldn't,* happen. He'd spent the past couple of days tightening the budget, talking to his people, getting everyone prepped and ready for the meeting with the engineers and the board next week. He'd planned to spend the rest of the weekend going over the presentation to the board to solidify the project's funding.

Cass whuffled and shoved her hair out of her face before curling her hand under her cheek.

Every thought of work faded. He watched her until he couldn't help but reach out and stroke her cheek. Soft, like peach skin, and flushed with sleep. Dark lashes fanned out. Her lips were red and still a little puffy from being kissed completely senseless. The upper swells of her breasts peeked above the covers, one dusky nipple exposed to the cool air.

Complicated or not, she was so damn beautiful she made his chest ache.

Eyes the color of deepest sapphire blinked open. The haze of sleep dissipated as she watched him watch her. And then she smiled. Slow and lazy, it was undeniably self-satisfied. "Hey."

Thirty seconds ago, he would have bet it all she couldn't get any sexier than she'd been last night. He would have lost his shirt. "Hey." Unable to stop himself, he stroked her cheek again. "How'd you sleep?"

She rubbed against him like a cat, stretching and groaning. "I haven't slept that well in I don't even remember how long." Glancing at him through those long lashes, she bit her bottom lip. "You?"

"Great, just not long enough."

Her gaze dropped. "Yeah. Sorry about that."

He curled a finger under her chin and lifted. "Ask me if I'd do anything differently."

She considered him as she continued worrying her lip. "Would you?"

He shook his head. "Uh-uh."

A small smile tipped up one corner of her mouth. "Rousing endorsement, that."

He laughed. "Sorry. Just got caught up looking at you." Shaking his head, he kissed her nose before rolling out of bed and yanking his jeans on. "I'm going to scavenge for some breakfast."

Cass sat up, the mass of her hair and sheet-creased skin making his cock stir again. He wanted nothing more than to shed his jeans and spend the day in bed with this woman, and that was a first. In fact, he couldn't remember the last time he'd spent the whole night with someone when it was a single fling. Shit. Talk about complicating things. He needed to get out of there.

"You okay? You look like someone just walked over your grave," she teased.

Eric dropped to the side of the bed and cradled his hands in his head. "I just need to get something to eat. Low blood sugar."

"No scavenging. There's this place down by the Market that makes phenomenal crepes." She crawled over to him and rested her hands on his shoulders. "Give me five minutes and we'll go." Giving him a light squeeze, she bounded out of bed.

There weren't words to protest or pass on the invitation, not when she was crossing the room in all her naked glory. With a quick smile over her shoulder, she disappeared into her walk-in closet.

The way he saw it, he had two choices. He could quietly collect his stuff and run, or he could pull himself together and go with the flow, at least for one more day. He stood, grabbed his shirt and slipped it on even as he searched for his shoes. They were in the foyer, and he shoved his feet in sans socks. They were cold, but he'd survive. His jacket hung on the coat tree, and he had to step over Cass's jeans and stilettos to get to it. Patting his pockets down, he found his keys and wallet.

"Dalton?"

"Out here, baby. Just getting my stuff together so I'd be ready when you are."

She rounded the corner and started down the hall toward him.

His breath clogged his chest.

Clad in skin-tight leggings, a long sweater and riding boots, hair in a loose topknot and her face free of makeup, she was gorgeous. Absolutely fucking gorgeous.

"Everything okay?"

Pulled in by her mere presence, he went to her, kicking last night's clothes out of the way. Wrapping her in his arms was as natural as breathing her in. The way the back of her head fit in his hand made him wonder if she'd been sculpted for him. And all that romantic nonsense reminded him he was in way over his head. He wanted to beat his chest like a damn gorilla that, for the moment, this woman was his. What he should have done was beat his head against the wall for his immeasurable stupidity. Their relationship couldn't go anywhere, and they both knew it. She was clearly successful at whatever she did while he was still taking his clothes off to make ends meet. The Chok Resort deal would make him, but until then? She was out of his league. He'd do well to remember that—after today.

He pulled her in closer and her eyes widened. "Seriously? Again?"

"I told you I wasn't ready for this to be over."

"That was before we—" she waved a free hand "—you know, like, five times."

He grinned. "You were counting. That's cute." Burying his hands in her hair, Eric tilted her head back and lowered his mouth to hers. Something huge roared inside him when she sighed and closed her eyes, giving herself to the moment, to the kiss, to him.

Eric would still go because he didn't want things to grow complicated. After he finished kissing her.

CASS'S TOES CURLED in her boots as Dalton's tongue delved into her mouth in a sexual parody she had no doubt would become reality if she didn't stop him. But she didn't want to stop him. She wanted him to pull her beneath his delicious weight or bend her over the kitchen counter or press her up against the wall again. Something, anything, that would allow her access to his body. Last night had been the best sexual experience of her life, and she wasn't ready for it to end. They'd both been clear sex was all they wanted, and she'd half expected him to sneak out after she fell asleep. Opening her eyes and finding him watching her had been the best way she could have started her day. She could hold on to the fantasy for a few more hours.

He nipped her bottom lip as he pulled back and searched her eyes. "Where'd you go?"

She shrugged. "Lost in thought, I guess."

"I'm not doing my job if you can still think. You're sure you want to go out?"

His job... Yeah, that was part of the problem, wasn't it?

"I need food and a little fresh air."

Tracing the pad of one thumb over her lips, he considered her. "What are your plans?"

"Plans?"

"For the rest of the day."

She cleared her throat and stepped away, unable to clear her mind with him touching her. "I don't really have any. I need to spend a little time at the office getting some stuff together for a huge presentation next week, but otherwise…" Shrugging, she picked her coat up off the floor. "Nothing."

He waggled his brows. "Then there's no rush to go out."

Cass grabbed her purse and dug out her keys. "That means there's plenty of time left in the day if we *do* go out."

"Fine," he said on a sigh.

"C'mon, Eeyore." Hooking her arm through his, she opened the door and led him out. "Let's find sustenance and bemoan the fact we're in public, in clothes, behaving like reasonable adults and not in bed, naked, acting like porn stars."

He followed her out, grinning. "Porn stars. Sounds fun."

"You didn't hear another word I said, did you?"

The elevator doors opened on a hiss at the same moment he answered. "Hey, I got the important part. We're coming back after breakfast to act like porn stars."

Her elderly, ultra-reserved neighbor, Mrs. Sliff, stopped halfway out of the car and arched a brow as she gaped at Dalton.

"Mrs. Sliff." Cass couldn't decide whether to die on the spot or turn in her notice to vacate the premises.

"Darling, if I had a gorgeous young man who offered to play porn star with me, you'd have to send six dangerously delicious firemen to drag my wrinkled ass out of my apartment." The woman winked at Dalton and worked it as she walked away from him.

"She might get her wish for the firemen," he muttered, watching her go. "She's going to throw out a hip walking like that."

Already in the elevator and pressing the lobby button repeatedly, Cass reached out and dragged Dalton in. The minute the doors closed, she collapsed against the wall in fits of laughter. She'd lived here for four years and not once had she exchanged more than cool greetings with the old woman. One glimpse of Dalton and the woman had been more than conversational. Cass couldn't breathe. Tears streamed down her face as Dalton watched her with open curiosity and undisguised amusement.

"Is she really that bad?"

Cass could only hiccup and nod as she wiped the tears from her cheeks. "I'm ruined. I'll never be able to look at her again without remembering this conversation."

Dalton closed the distance between them.

She had to tip her head up to meet his stare. Something dark and wanting lurked in his eyes and made her shiver. "What?"

He swept a thumb along her jaw. "You're so damn beautiful."

A flush of pleasure made her bury her face in his chest. "Thank you, but really? It was just a lucky hand in the cosmic genetics poker game. I had nothing to do with it."

He cupped her face and lifted it. "Fine. I'll send your parents a thank-you note."

A pang of age-old hurt made her lungs burn. "Don't waste your time. They can't be bothered with social niceties unless you're in their circle."

Dropping his hand from her face, he considered her. "And what circle is that?"

"Can we talk about something else?" she asked, closing her eyes.

"Sure, but you wear your beauty well, Cass. No one is responsible for that but you." He stepped back as the doors opened.

She wondered if he'd used that line on any of his other clients. But even if he had, so what? She wasn't asking for a commitment. He was with her now, and he made her feel good; that was all that mattered.

Deliberately, she took Dalton's hand and started across the lobby. No one had to know he was a stripper. And if no one knew, no one could pass the news on to her clients and associates. Her secret was safe. And if her secret was safe, so was her reputation. Pretty much.

What a convoluted mess. It bothered her she'd had the best night of her life with someone whose profession could damage her career. And if her dad found out, he would blow a—

"Excuse me, ma'am?"

She stopped so abruptly Dalton crashed into her and drove her forward a few steps. Apprehension curled through her stomach as she turned to face the concierge, disturbed to find it was the nosiest of the bunch. "Yes?"

"A courier delivered this roughly an hour ago." She held out the large envelope as she sized Dalton up. "How was Ms. Sivern's party last night?"

"Lovely, thank you." She let go of Dalton's hand and closed the distance to the counter to accept the proffered envelope. Apprehension turned to sour dread at the sight of the return address. Jameson & Whitman, LLC. Whatever her father had sent over couldn't be good. It never was. But when he hired a courier to deliver the news, it meant he wanted something.

Cass absently handed her keys to Dalton, never tak-

ing her eyes off the envelope. "Would you mind bringing the car down?"

He considered her, his face becoming an emotional
void. "Sure." He took the keys and stalked off.

She didn't miss the edge to his tone, but this was something she couldn't discuss. Not at this point. Slipping
outside, she sank onto the nearest bench and picked at
the corner of the manila envelope. She sliced her finger. "Damn it." Working around the deep paper cut, she
fished out a single piece of heavy letterhead with shaking
hands. It took two passes to process the handwritten note.

Metropolitan restaurant, 8:00 p.m. prompt.
Dress accordingly.
Primary point of discussion: EPA clearance of
Chok Resort plan
—DJameson

"I'm fine," she whispered to herself, swallowing
around the heavy emotion wedged in her throat and
nearly choking. "I'm fine."

But that was a lie. *How the hell did my father find out
about the EPA clearance in less than twenty-four hours?*
It made no sense. Not unless he had someone on the inside. But would it be on the EPA's side or... Her stomach tightened and she thought, for just a second, she was
going to vomit. No. It wouldn't be someone inside Preservations. No way. She couldn't accept the possibility.

Digging her cell out of her bag with numb fingers, she
tapped in Gwen's number.

Halfway through the third ring the other woman answered, her voice heavy with sleep. "Why are you calling me so early?"

"I...I..." Cass closed her eyes and forced a deep breath into lungs as rigid as rawhide.

"Cass?" Gwen's voice was suddenly sharp. "What happened? Are you okay? Did he hurt you?"

"What? No. No, I'm..." She started to answer "fine" by rote, but it would have been yet another lie, and she couldn't stand liars.

Covers rustled in the background and a deep voice grunted in protest. "I'm coming over."

Clearing her throat, Cass tried again. "No. Listen, I'm fine. I just needed to hear your voice for a second." She breathed deep, the smell of damp earth and evergreen tickling her nose. "My father sent me an 'invitation' to dinner at the Metropolitan tonight. Eight sharp. He managed to discover that the EPA cleared us."

"Shit. How?"

"I have no idea. But it's our 'talking point' tonight."

"He's going to try and intimidate you the second you're alone together."

"Yeah, well, he can bring it. I intend to find out who told him before it was publicly announced. He's lining the right pockets to get the right information, and has been since he lost the bid for the development." She hesitated, nibbling at a hangnail. "I don't want to think he's paying someone in our house."

Gwen sighed. "I don't, either. If we find out the leak is from one of ours, we'll have to let the person go."

"We might have to press charges, Gwen."

"It doesn't have to go that far, does it?"

"Depends on what my father brings to the table tonight." A shadow passed over her, and she looked up to find Dalton staring down at her.

He arched a brow and tipped his head toward the car. "Ready?"

She signaled for him to give her a minute, and at the same time she shoved off the bench and wandered a few steps away. "I'll let you know what happens. Chances are I'm going to be late to our celebration at Bathtub Gin."

"Just try to get there before midnight. Was that Dalton?"

Cass took a deep breath, smiling softly. "Yeah."

Gwen squealed and shouted at Dave, "Cass got laid!"

Her grin widened. "You have no idea."

"You owe me details!"

Looking over her shoulder, she found Dalton leaned up against her car watching her. A hard shiver cartwheeled down her spine. "Later. I have to go."

She thumbed the phone off before Gwen could respond.

Stepping under the portico again, she wadded up the envelope and invitation before shoving them into the trash.

7

ERIC SETTLED INTO the passenger seat as Cass disconnected her call. Whatever had been in the envelope had upset her. No, *upset* was too mild a word. The content had thoroughly pissed her off. Eric was pissed off himself for being so unequivocally dismissed from her life. He had no right to expect she'd include him, but to be sent for the car? Not cool.

Cass slipped into the driver's seat and slammed her door. Instead of putting the car in gear, though, she fiddled with the radio for a moment before finally asking, "Are you still hungry?"

"I could eat."

A single nod was all the response he got. She shifted the car into gear and pulled away from the apartment building, turning onto Broadway. Rain drummed on the car roof. The *whoosh-snap* tempo of the windshield wipers increased as the rain grew heavier. Traffic was congested, even for a Saturday morning. They cruised past Pike's Place and continued north in silence until he couldn't take it any longer.

"I thought we were grabbing crepes near the Market."

"Yeah." She shot him a quick glance. "I decided I'm

feeling a little less refined, a little more carnivorous than earlier."

"Okay, spill. What was in the envelope?"

His seat belt locked up when she hit the brakes at a crosswalk. Her hands strangled the steering wheel, twisting forward and back hard enough that the leather creaked in protest. "It was family stuff." She pressed her palm to her forehead, an unfamiliar, rueful smile coaxing out her one dimple. "And by 'family stuff,' I mean it was a bullshit note from my father."

"Sounds like you don't have the best relationship with him."

"I'd have to have *a* relationship before it could be deemed good or bad." Sighing, she switched lanes and rolled her head side to side. "Sorry. He's a sore subject with me. Always has been, always will be."

"If you want to talk about it, I'm game."

"What's the catch?"

His brows drew together as he tried to figure out where she was going. "Catch?"

This time her grin was far more familiar as she pulled into a park space along the street and shut the engine off. "You're amazing in bed, stuck around till morning and you're willing to talk. If you don't disclose a fault or two, you're going to screw up my universally negative view of the male species."

Eric snorted. "Such a pessimist."

"That's fair."

"What's fair about that?"

"I *am* a pessimist. Just ask Gwen. In my defense, it's an inherited trait." She pulled her hair down and shook it out before winding it up into a careless, sexy topknot again. "Even if that does sound a little foolish."

"And you never sound foolish?" he teased gently.

The vulnerability in her gaze shuttered, and she sat back. "Being proven a fool is to be proven weak, and I can't afford to be weak. Not right now."

"Is that why you threw out the envelope?"

"I do everything I can to ensure my family lives their lives and I live mine. If ne'er the twain shall meet, all the better."

There was bitterness there, but heartache, as well. It called to his, like to like. Together they were so different yet so similar, both longing for one thing—respect and acceptance.

She blinked, and that hard part of her that had peaked out faded. "Have you been to Mecca before?"

"Mecca?" He peered at the rain-blurred building in front of them to buy a little time to catch up. "I've heard of it but haven't been here."

"You know, you could lose your Seattle residency for never having paid homage to the Holy Grail of diners." Grabbing the door handle, she shoved out of the car and sprinted for the front door.

Eric raced after her, catching her just under the portico. He swung her into his arms. Wide blue eyes stared up at him, lovely and once again unguarded. He lowered his mouth to hers, moving gently against the seam of her lips until she opened to him. She wound her fingers through is hair. Tongues clashed in a sudden blast of heat he hadn't been prepared for. Sheltered from the worst of the rain, they fell into each other.

He wanted to get to know her, to discover her favorite flavor of ice cream and the type of toothpaste in her bathroom and which side of the bed she normally slept on. He wanted her to trust him, to give him the chance to prove to her that she was amazing, unique, wonderful. Cherished.

His phone vibrated in his pocket. He started to reach for it and changed his mind.

Whatever it was could wait. Today, he was just Dalton Reeves, the guy who was having a hot, amazing affair with a hot, amazing woman.

BREAKFAST HAD BEEN an easy affair aside from the cost of eating out. They'd talked and laughed and carefully danced around heavier topics as they sipped some of the best coffee he'd had in ages while sharing waffles, bacon, sausage, eggs and hash browns. Her foot absently caressed the inside of his ankle as she chatted. It drove him insane. All he could think about was the blue nail polish she wore beneath the casually chic outfit. Such a small thing, yet so telling. She was more than the sum of first impressions and exchanged pleasantries. Passion and humor and loyalty—she had them and more.

And yet, the pessimistic side of him wondered what she thought of him, or at least the tiny part he was choosing to show her.

The very idea of revealing more made his movements clumsy enough he knocked his coffee over. "Shit! Sorry."

She scooted away from the table at the same time she grabbed a handful of napkins and began mopping up. "No harm, no foul."

Eric flagged down the waiter.

The guy was cool about it, grabbing a few rags and scooping sopping napkins onto an empty plate. "Happens all the time, man."

His phone buzzed against his hip again. Digging it out of his pocket, he saw it was his brother. So much for his Eric Reeves holiday. "Excuse me just a second." Turning, he headed toward the front of the diner.

His little brother, Blake, had sent three texts. The first

said, Need to talk to you. That one had come in while he was caught up with Cass on the sidewalk. The second, Sooner would be better. The third simply, Serious, bro.

He pulled his brother's information up and dialed. The phone rang several times and then dumped him into voice mail. "What's so urgent you blow up my phone with texts and then can't pick up when I call, man?" Tone light, he told Blake to call him back as soon as possible and disconnected.

A gentle hand slipped around his waist, teasing under his shirt hem. Fingernails scraped along his waistband. Sexual tension folded his desire into an origami flame that licked its way up from the base of his spine to the top of his skull. "If you're not my date, you should probably move along. She's incredibly territorial and has very sharp teeth and an extra thumb on one hand. Oh, and a peg leg she lost in a pirating accident. She's vicious."

Soft laughter vibrated against his back. "Unless she's got an eye patch and a parrot, I can take her."

He turned in her embrace and leaned back to look her over. "I don't know. You're pretty delectable but not all that scary. My money's on her."

"I'm scarier than I appear," she said, her bottom lip pouting prettily. "Besides, she sounds like she should be kept on a leash. Throw her over and come home with me. I already paid the bill."

Muscles along his spine tightened. "You didn't have to do that."

"I only did it because it meant I could run away with you faster." She ran a hand up and down his arm. "Dalton?"

Eric forced himself to relax. It meant nothing that she'd dropped nine bucks on him. Nine bucks he didn't have to spare at the moment. To cover his discomfort, he grabbed her hand and pulled her into the rain.

She laughed, pounding through puddles at his side.

They reached the car together. He swung her off the street and over the worst of the gutter flow, depositing her on the sidewalk with a flourish. "Can't have you getting those sexy feet wet."

Shoving hair out of her face, confusion marred her brow. "Sexy feet?"

He planted his hands on his hips and let his chin fall to his chest. "The blue nail polish. It's sexy as hell." Her sharp exhale made him peer at her. "What?"

"Just… You noticed my toes."

Embarrassment crawled up the back of his neck and prickled along his nape. He shifted his gaze to an obscure point over her shoulder. "It's not a big deal, Cass."

"Let's go back to my place." Her husky tone made him glance at her sharply.

"I should grab some dry clothes."

She licked her lips as she stepped in close and gazed up at him. "You won't need them. Trust me."

And damn if he didn't. Taking her car keys, he helped her into the passenger's seat and jogged to the driver's side.

"A little chauvinistic, isn't it, assuming the man is more capable behind the wheel?" She fished a few napkins out of the glove box and handed him some to dry his face.

"Nope."

"Why's that?" she asked, eyes narrowing.

"It's a matter of safety."

"Safety?" Crossing her arms under her breasts, she arched a brow. "Go on."

"If I don't have my hands on the wheel, they're going

to be all over you. The probability of an accident increases exponentially because you *would* be distracted. By letting me drive, you're actually performing your civic duty by forcing me to focus on the road."

Her laughter was soft and feminine and caressed every male cell in his body.

"Heaven knows I wouldn't want to be responsible for vehicular carnage."

"The city of Seattle and its residents thank you."

She shook her head and absently waved a hand. "Home, James."

He pulled into traffic on cue.

The trip back to the Harbormaster apartments was comfortably quiet, his mind so full of the woman at his side he nearly forgot about everything else. When he was with Cass, it was easy to pretend he'd found the kind of success he'd dreamed of for so long. It was easy to imagine having a life where he could pursue a woman like her.

He traced the heel of her hand with his thumb. So many opportunities right in front of him. If he could just make enough money to close the social gap between him and this woman, if he could write a check for his brother's tuition without worrying about it clearing, if he could afford to pay himself a reasonable salary and be able to quit stripping, he'd be happy. And in this moment, with her, all of that seemed possible.

Settling their joined hands on the console, he reveled in the fact that, for the first time in a very long time, he didn't feel alone. She was here, now, chasing away the darkness that clawed at him and replacing it with the realization she was the first breath of hope he'd had in what seemed like forever. Even if she damned him later for it, he'd take whatever he could get.

CASS FOUGHT THE increasing urge to squirm with every traffic light that delivered them closer to her apartment. She might have kissed Dalton in public minutes ago, but no one knew them. Knew *him*. They were just some innocuous couple kissing in the rain. But once they got to the apartment complex, though, she might run into someone she knew, someone she'd have to introduce Dalton to.

Shame pushed her to slide lower in her seat. *Dress it up a thousand ways, you know what your problem is. He's a stripper.* And that irked her. Not that it bothered her that he took his clothes off for a living, but that she reacted the way she did. She didn't want to be that person. Behind closed doors, or in little dives where no one she socialized with hung out, she could pretend it was all okay, pretend she was urbane and chic and fine with everything. But in potentially social situations? Situations where she might run into peers or competitors? Even— or especially—her family? "Hi. This is Dalton Chase. We're lovers. He's a stripper."

And yet, it *was* a valid concern. Much as she hated it, she was smart enough to realize that there were double standards in business; what would pass in a man's social life would be humiliating in a woman's.

Still, her worries made her feel more like her father's daughter than ever before—more worried about perception than anything else.

And what about happiness? her conscience whispered. *What's that worth to you?*

That might be the biggest question of all. There were a thousand excuses she could make to bow out of this thing with Dalton, but none of them was going to absolve her from being a jerk for the sake of her business. She sank even lower in her seat.

"Go much lower and your shoulders are going to

get wedged in your ears." When she didn't answer, he chanced a longer glance despite traffic. "Hey. What's wrong?"

"Nothing." Shoving herself out of the wallowing position, she plucked her wet sweater away from her chest and shivered. "Ready to get out of this thing."

"Trust me. I'm ready to help you with that."

If he knew what she was thinking, he wouldn't be. He'd ditch her. She wouldn't be able to blame anyone but herself for his exit stage left. Why did she overcomplicate things? Why couldn't she just choose happiness? After all, they'd both agreed this was a short-term thing that didn't require analyzing. It just was.

He turned into the Harbormaster's parking garage without comment.

Her hand tightened around his as she nodded at the valet. "He'll park the car."

Dalton's fingers tapped out a rapid beat against the steering wheel as he stared out the windshield. "You know, the concierge on duty is the same one who was on last night when I came in."

Cass's stomach somersaulted around her abdomen in a wild, championship-worthy routine. Burying her fist below her diaphragm, she nodded. "Yeah?"

"Yeah. Why don't I park the car and go in a side door so she doesn't get nosy about me hanging around?"

She was embarrassed to be relieved. "If you want."

"It would be easier for both of us." He paused, seeming to consider his words. "The club might get a little testy about me spending the weekend with a client, and I can't afford that." His voice, low and fervent, held a desperation she couldn't quite interpret.

Closing her eyes and drawing a deep breath, she shoved her hands in her sweater pockets. "You can't afford for this to turn into something? What does that mean?" She stole a quick glance in his direction.

"It means I could lose my job." Stepping out of the car, he slipped around to open her door for her. He hooked a finger under her chin and nudged it gently so she peered up into his face. "I need this job, Cass. It's not a matter of want."

And that's what she was—a matter of want. Wrapping her arms around her middle, Cass nodded. "Take the keys and head in the side door. I'll go through the lobby."

"Thank you, Cass. It's…easier for me this way."

She stared at him, standing gorgeous and wet under the portico. "That's not something you often do, though, is it? Take the easy route?"

He winced. "For what it's worth, no, I usually end up with more on my shoulders than I can manage. Atlas, I'm not."

One corner of her mouth fluttered up. "See you upstairs."

"Don't take too long," he teased, leaning in to give her a short, thorough kiss.

"No worries. I'm efficient. Stairs are right over there." She tossed him her key ring. "You'll need the key to get in if you beat me."

He laughed, turning toward the side entrance. "The cardio will be good for me."

"I may beat *you* to the top."

"Is that a challenge?" he asked, his face alight with amusement.

"Consider that the gauntlet being thrown. I hereby challenge you to a race to the top."

"Challenge accepted." Spinning around, he took off for the stairs.

Cass strode toward the main entrance, through the

giant glass doors and was halfway across the lobby when her personal hell called out.

"Cass?"

Every hair on her body stood on end as she slowed to a stop and faced not only the concierge but also her father's right-hand man. He stood tall and straight, his suit impeccable and a huge bouquet of wrapped roses cradled in one arm.

"Marcus," she said, inclining her head.

"Your father requests you arrive at dinner at seventhirty instead, as he's had an issue arise."

Cass huffed out a heavy breath. "And you needed to deliver this message in person? A simple phone call would have sufficed."

"I wanted to see you, Cassidy." He stepped closer, unbuttoning the single button of his designer suit. "These are for you, beautiful." He handed her the flowers with smooth surety even as his dark brown eyes filled with regret. Perfectly sculpted eyebrows settled together on an admirably handsome face and conveyed the perfect level of concern and remorse. Everything about Marcus seemed designed, and it irritated her. Not a single scar. Not a single tattoo. Not a single blemish. He wasn't real, and during their short-lived relationship, he had taught her she valued authenticity. "I've missed you."

"I appreciate you delivering the message, but you could have called. Rest assured, I'll be on time to dinner."

"And on my comment that I've missed you?" he pressed, his tone neutral and so reminiscent of her father's she fought the shudder that ran though her body.

"Thank you for the sentiment." She shifted, anxious to end this conversation. "I'm sure I'll see you tonight."

"Undoubtedly." He stepped even closer, invading her

space as he reached out to trace her cheek with his fingertips. "I'm glad you accepted my invitation."

She backed away. "Oh, no. No, no, no. This was an invitation from my father, not you."

"I'm part of the evening's discussions," he answered with smooth control. "Seven-thirty tonight, Cassidy." Pivoting, he strolled from the building without a backward glance.

Mirroring his actions, she spun and headed for the elevators, all thoughts of the race with Dalton gone.

8

ERIC STOOD INSIDE Cass's apartment waiting for her to make it past the concierge. Shame burned up the back of his neck. He'd never let anyone fight his battles for him, and he wasn't about to start now. He'd deal with the fall-out from the club if he had to.

Yanking the door open, he found Cass standing in the hallway, hand raised to knock.

"Where were you?" he asked, taking in her wide eyes, pale complexion and the $200 worth of roses she held in her arms. "Shopping?"

"No," she said on a bitter laugh. "Fighting off an overly attentive suitor. Feel better?"

Jealousy churned in his belly. "Ironically, no."

Then she looked up at him with eyes so shadowed he realized he hadn't even scratched the surface of who this dynamic woman really was. He pulled her into his arms, and the sweet crush of rose petals wrapped around them as he held her.

"What happened, baby?"

For the longest time she didn't say anything. Then, in a low voice, she said, "Just a guy who works for my dad. Thinks I'm part of the compensation package, I guess."

The joke held too much truth to be funny.

Eric's arms tightened around her. He was furious he hadn't been there, enraged he had left her to defend herself.

"Trouble breathing down here, Dalton."

He forced himself to meet her gaze as he relaxed his grip on her.

"Thanks." Wiggling an arm free, she traced the deep V between his brows. "What's this?"

"I should have been there, Cass. You shouldn't have had to deal with that on your own." He choked the sharp words out.

"It wasn't your responsibility."

"Bullshit."

"What makes you think I need you to take care of my problems?" she demanded, pulling away from him. "You're not my boyfriend."

The smell of roses intensified as she struggled a bit before he finally let her go. "That may be true, but I would've enjoyed it."

"You were doing so well. Don't go all caveman on me now."

"Caveman?"

"You know, dragging me around by the hair and making decisions for my well-being and all that shit. I've lived alone for years, handled jerks of every shape, size and color. I've got this. He might be a perfect catch according to my family's standards, but I'm not interested."

Fighting to keep his tone level, he met her stare. "A 'perfect catch,' meaning he has money and prestige and social position, I assume."

"Pretty much." Turning, she started down the hall toward the kitchen. "I'm going to put these in water."

"You're keeping them?"

"Yeah. They can't help that they were delivered by an asshole."

An unfamiliar feeling burned through him. He was *not* jealous of the stranger. Why should he be? He'd only just met Cass and they'd had a great time. Things had been great—and casual. Right up until the mystery man had shown up. Watching her ass sway as she stalked down the hall in a Fashion Week–worthy walk, his fingers twitched. He wanted his hands on her. He wanted his mouth on her. He wanted…her.

He silently followed her. She yanked a cabinet open in the kitchen and dropped the flowers on the island. But instead of a vase, she retrieved a shot glass and a bottle of tequila. Pouring with shaking hands, she spilled the liquor all over the counter.

Eric stepped in close and closed a hand over hers. "A little early for a drink, don't you think?"

"I never do this." She looked up at him with impossibly wide eyes. *"Never."*

"Don't start now."

The tequila bottle connected with the granite countertop with a sharp crack when she set it down. "You're right. I just… I have to…" She swallowed and wiped a bead of sweat from her brow. "I don't even know," she said on a desperate laugh. "He scared me, Dalton."

"Did he hurt you?" He fought the urge to get the guy's name and kill him slowly. That wasn't what she needed.

"No. Just rattled me."

Eric gently drew her into his arms. They stood there, chest to chest, her heart beating out a wild rhythm while his hammered violently against his rib cage.

He wanted to give her sweet words of reassurance, but the cost of those words was potential heartache. Everything he longed to say to her could come back to him tenfold. But he could give her one thing, though....

He pulled the thick elastic band out of her hair and let the caramel mass fall around her shoulders. Her hair was silk against his hands as he ran his fingers through the loose curls. Fisting her hair, he pulled her head back and reveled in her gasp. Tender skin gave under his teeth's sharp nips, though he never bit her very hard. This wasn't about that kind of play. This was about helping her forget the madness of the moment just past, the impending dinner with her father and, above all, obliterating the mystery man's words and actions.

She clung to his shoulders, her nails digging into him with desperation. "Please," she breathed.

Nibbling and licking his way up her neck, he traced the shell of her ear with the tip of his tongue. "Please what, Cass?"

Turning her chin aside, she gave him full access to the lush column of her neck.

To hell with what this moment was and wasn't. He closed his teeth over the juncture of neck and shoulder and bit her.

"Dalton," she moaned, sagging in his embrace.

As he caught her, he acknowledged there were times his strength came in handy. Never had it made him feel so alive, though. One lithe leg wrapped around his thigh as she moved against him, rubbing her sex against the hard ridge of his erection. Every hip-rolling thrust, every sigh and gasp and sound of encouragement pushed him closer to the tenuous brink of control. Deep blue eyes stared up at him from beneath heavy lids. Long, capable fingers laced together behind his head and pulled him close.

Their lips came together in a rough joining. He slanted his mouth over hers and worked at her, swallowing her small sounds of pleasure. She tugged him in tighter. Then she opened her mouth to him, darting her tongue out to trace over his. She tasted faintly of syrup and bacon. Her damp clothes smelled like rain and fabric softener and a scent he already recognized as all her. Long lashes fluttered closed as the kiss deepened, pulling him under as surely as she herself sank.

Strong, capable fingers massaged his neck and tangled in his hair. She went up on her toes and pulled him in closer still, meeting him more than halfway.

He let her come.

A soft, hungry sound escaped her.

His answer was silent but unmistakable. Grabbing her around the waist, he spun and set her on the island, parking himself between her legs. He tugged her ass forward so she hovered on the counter's edge. She'd have to choose to trust him not to let her fall, and he wanted that trust. Needed it. Bad.

Her legs wrapped around his waist and she arched into him. The wanton movement slid her core over the head of his cock.

Eric thrust forward. Her leggings stretched and pulled against the strain of his arousal and created an erotic temptation he couldn't ignore. The lush curves of her hips fit his hands as if she'd been made for him and him alone. He pulled her forward, encouraging her through heated kisses and wordless instruction to ride the hard ridge of his erection until every caress dragged a small sound of hunger from his throat or a purr of approval from her chest.

Cass leaned back, whipped her sweater over her head and unhooked her bra. Nipples beaded with arousal, she hissed as she ran a hand over one breast, lifting for his mouth.

He suckled her, rolling the tiny pearl of flesh between his lips and flicking it with the tip of his tongue.

"Dalton." She fisted his hair, dragging him closer. "Feels so good."

"Boots." He moved to her mouth and kissed her deep before breaking away. Cupping her face, he forced her to focus on him. "Off."

Toeing them off was the work of a moment, and her leggings followed quickly.

Eric's brain fuzzed out. *She'd gone commando.* His balls tightened hard and fast, the burn of pleasure spreading through him as his body focused on the orgasm it wouldn't be denied. Not now. When he ran his hands over her silken skin and laid her back across the cold granite, goose bumps broke out over her arms. He breathed across her bare belly, reveling in the evidence of her arousal. It was a temptation all its own.

Dipping low, he ran his tongue along the seam of her sex.

She bowed off the countertop with a harsh cry, hands scrabbling for purchase as he tasted the most feminine parts of her.

Shaft aching, he couldn't wait any longer. He rolled her over on the island, sending the fruit bowl crashing to the ground. He'd replace it. Hell, he'd get her five of them. Later. He had to have her. Now.

Pulling her toward him by the hips, he pinned her thighs together by planting his legs on each side of hers.

She spread her arms and gripped the edges of the counter.

"Cass." Her name was little more than an invocation, a plea for absolution because he was going to use her, and hard. He drove into her with a single stroke.

She shouted and pushed back against him, trying to gain leverage.

Eric wasn't about to cede control. No, he would take her to the very edge with every ounce of skill he had and then launch her over into that beautiful free fall. The pace he set was ruthless. For every thrust, she pushed back to meet him. Her hair hung loose, and he reached forward to fist it off her face and pull her head back. "So damn beautiful," he ground out.

His orgasm burned through him like a dry fuse running to a powder keg. When he lost it, the results were going to be spectacular. He didn't want to go without her, though. With his free hand, he reached around her and, finding her clit, manipulated her in time with their lovemaking.

She tightened around him in throbbing waves, clamping down on him like a glove that was suddenly two sizes too small. Her muscles fluttered and tugged at his cock without mercy.

That was his breaking point.

The orgasm blew through him, but he continued to drive into her even as he let go, his shout ricocheting around the kitchen. Pleasure crested and rose again, drawing him higher with every pulse of release before withdrawing and leaving him weak-kneed and sheened in sweat.

He leaned over her, bracing his shaking arms against the counter. "Holy shit."

Slipping an arm around her waist, he sank to the floor as gracefully as he could manage and propped himself against the cabinets. She curled into his lap, and he held her close. No matter what else had happened today, this was right.

This was right.

THIRTY MINUTES LATER Cass was showered and feeling a little more in control. Okay, not so much "in control" as she was still blissed out from the amazing orgasm Dalton had delivered. It was more than just the physical pleasure, though. She'd opened up to him, and he'd understood. And for that reason, he had to go.

The shower shut off and Dylan stepped out, obliterating any coherent thought. She'd seen him naked, but there was something about seeing him standing in her bathroom, water droplets navigating the peaks and valleys of his torso, his hair plastered back, his green eyes framed by dark spiked lashes, that simply made her stop breathing.

He rubbed a hand over his jaw. "I need to shave."

"I'd let you borrow my razor, but it would probably tear your face up it's so old. I generally get waxed."

Those deep green eyes darkened as they roved over her towel-wrapped body. "I know."

Something entirely feminine fluttered in her belly.

"Hand me a towel?"

The urge to toss him hers was almost overwhelming, but she knew it would lead to sex. And she had things she had to do this afternoon that required clothes—like prepare for the biggest presentation of her life. Sighing, she grabbed a fresh towel out of the basket near her feet and tossed it to him.

He snagged it and, after drying off, wrapped it around his waist. "I don't suppose you have an extra toothbrush?"

Cass dug through one of the vanity drawers and pulled out a freebie from the dentist, still in its cellophane. She handed it over with a small smile. "Best I can do."

"Perfect." He opened it, loaded it with toothpaste and began to brush. "The mystery man seems a li'l proprietary about you."

"He'd like to be."

"Relationship gone wrong?"

"'Relationship' implies there was something between us beyond his overactive imagination." Her words were clipped, almost cold.

Rinsing his mouth, he laid the toothbrush beside the sink. "Fair enough."

Clarification seemed prudent. "You and I hit the sheets in record time, but that's not my typical speed. He wanted it to be. I objected. He hasn't taken it well."

"You don't owe me an explanation, Cass."

She didn't want to owe him so much as she wanted him to know more about her, the real her. She'd already given him more of a glimpse of the true Cassidy Jameson than she'd given any other man, and it stung a little that he was so laissez-faire about their relationship. She knew she shouldn't expect anything more, knew it was foolishness to set herself up to fall for a man she didn't know, but...

But maybe he didn't have to leave.

A sense of absolute conviction marched up her spine. She wanted to understand what it was she felt when he held her, what it was he stirred in her body when he loved her. She wanted to understand him. What could it hurt to have him stay for one more day? The idea thrilled her.

Reaching around him, she grabbed his toothbrush and dropped it in the porcelain holder where she kept hers.

Dalton watched her, quietly considering. Then he smiled. "Well, okay." Running his fingers through her damp curls, his gaze roamed over her face.

"Have breakfast with me."

"We already ate."

"Tomorrow," she said, her breath quickening as he

stroked a thumb over her creased brow. "Have breakfast with me tomorrow."

When he didn't respond, she settled her hands at his waist, his chiseled abs tightening. "Ticklish?"

"You'll never get me to admit it."

Biting her bottom lip, she dug her fingers into his sides.

Dalton shouted and danced out of her way, the towel slipping as low as it could around his hips without falling off. "Not playing nice, Cass. I retaliate."

Palms out, she held out her hands in the universal sign for stop. "Truce. I have to go into the office and get a few things done this afternoon, then there's dinner with my father at the Metropolitan. I also have a little employee gathering at Bathtub Gin tonight. But after that?"

He ran his hand around the back of his neck and pulled hard enough that his muscles shook under the strain. Taking a deep breath, he looked up at her. "The Metropolitan, huh? Must be a big deal, dinner with your dad."

She considered him, taking in the tight lines around his eyes and the way his mouth went from lush to a hard, flat line between breaths. "No. Just dinner."

Dropping his arm, he rolled his head from side to side. "Later is probably best for me anyway since I have obligations tonight."

"Obligations." The flat word landed between them.

"Yeah. I have to work tonight."

The urge to ask him not to go tumbled to the tip of her tongue, but it was his job, and she had to get over her hang-up about what he did for a living. Fighting to cover the awkward conversational lull, she arched a brow and crossed her arms under her breasts. "Well, thank God that's all it is," she teased. "For a second I was afraid you were going to tell me you had a major jewel heist that was going to keep you tied up later than normal."

"Silly girl. That's not until Thursday night." He closed the distance between them and pulled her into a tight embrace. The intimacy of the moment—him holding her and she simply being held—made her breath catch and her heart tip toward him.

Sagging into him, she sighed.

His arms tightened. "You okay?"

"So long as we're still not headed for heartache, I'm cool."

His thumb stilled. "I wouldn't hurt you, Cass."

"People hurt each other all the time," she murmured, slipping from his embrace and heading to her closet.

He followed, stopping to lean on the doorjamb as she flipped through possible outfits for the evening. "Not everything ends badly."

She glanced over her shoulder, fighting to conjure a coy smile. "Ah, but everything ends." Shifting her attention to her clothes, she silently cursed herself for letting the pessimist in her surge to the surface and gain a voice.

Warm hands settled on her bare shoulders and pulled her into a solid torso. "If you want assurances this won't end, I can't give you that. But if you want assurances that I won't intentionally hurt you? Those I *can* give you."

"I don't need assurances, Dalton." She faced him, her expression friendly but intentionally closed down. "I appreciate the offer, but I'm old enough to know life doesn't offer guarantees. Whatever this is between us, it will run its course. We'll deal with whatever happens."

Eyes cooling a bit, he stepped back. "Are you always so—"

"Practical?" An arched brow silently dared him to challenge her. "Yes. I am."

He crossed an arm over his chest and grasped his opposite shoulder. "I wouldn't call it 'practical,' but it's good to know anyway."

Blindly grabbing the same little black dress she'd discarded the night before, she angled way past him and went to her lingerie drawer. "If it's not practical, what is it?" she called over her shoulder.

Those familiar hands caught her off balance and spun her, pulling her towel free as he hauled her forward. They crashed together, skin to skin, towels long gone. One hand wrapped around the back of her neck as the other held her to him. "Look at me."

Her face rose of its own volition even as her pride bristled at the command.

He lowered his face so close to hers that she had a hard time focusing on his mouth when he spoke. "It's not practical, Cass. It's demeaning. You're stripping away the beauty of discovering each other. Cut me a little slack in the predetermination department."

"Predetermination department?"

"You've already decided I'm going to disappoint you in some way—maybe I already have by the very nature of how we met. But until I really screw up, don't look forward to the event so anxiously you make it happen."

The observation struck far too close to home for her. She pulled against his hold until he let go. "You sound like a psychologist, not a Beaux Hommes man."

His face shuttered. "I didn't realize you held the two in such disparate esteem."

"I don't."

Dalton snorted. "Save it, Cass." He went for his still-damp jeans, pulling them on and toweling his hair relatively dry. "It might surprise you to know that one of my best friends is also a 'Beaux Hommes man' and he, ironically, just finished his Ph.D. in psychology." He shoved his arms down his shirtsleeves and pulled the Henley over his head. "Being a stripper doesn't make me stupid."

She held the dress over herself. "I never said that."

"Didn't you?"

"Dalton…" Pulse racing, she stepped toward him. "Don't leave. Not like this."

Brows drawn, he glanced over at her. "Like what?"

"Angry."

"I *am* angry." He considered her carefully, a riot of emotions racing across his face. "But that doesn't mean this is over." Closing the distance between them, he pulled her into his arms. "It's not over, Cass. Far from it. I do have to go, though."

"Come with me tonight to Bathtub Gin."

"I can't."

The pass on her invitation, delivered so quickly, stung. At the same time, the invitation had been impulsive and far too dangerous.

Something on her face must have given away the battle she waged internally, the very personal fight to find her balance with him without putting herself out there too far. He leaned one hip against her dresser and pulled her in close, resting his chin atop her head. "I can't," he repeated. "I really do have to work." Before she could say anything, he pressed his lips to hers, the kiss brief but intense. "Does the offer of breakfast still stand?"

She was reeling, unsure whether things were ending one moment or getting more serious the next. He was a basket of mixed signals, calling her out for being negative one moment and getting ready to leave her the next, and now, "Breakfast?"

"First meal of the day?" His grin was wicked. "Unless we repeat last night. Then it'll be brunch."

Her mouth twitched against her will as a smile bloomed. "You're insatiable."

"Right. It was all me."

"I'm a lady."

"In the boardroom, no doubt. But behind closed doors?" He lowered his mouth to her hers again, nibbling at her lips.

She opened to him with an involuntary sigh.

The kiss built in tension, the taste of him mingling with the familiar fresh flavor of her toothpaste. His lips were smooth but demanding. When he broke away, both of them were breathing heavily. "Behind closed doors, you're perfect."

"That's only because you've never seen me in the boardroom."

He laughed, hugged her and headed for the bedroom door. "I'll leave my cell number on your fridge. If you're free before one, come by the club. Otherwise, give me a call and we'll connect. Okay?"

The butterflies in her stomach told her there was only one answer that would suffice.

"See you tonight."

9

SLOGGING THROUGH THE entire presentation for the Sovereign Development project had taken every bit of the nine hours at the office Cass had allocated. Checking and double-checking geographical surveys, evaluating habitat impact and the viability of the natural conservation area the resort would sponsor, recalculating estimated slope post construction to ensure everything was right—it all took time.

In the end, though, she knew Preservations was ready. The owner of Sovereign would actually be at the meeting, and she was a little worried about that. She'd heard he was a real hard-ass about cost savings, but the solutions she and her team had proposed were the right ones. Maybe not the cheapest, but the EPA clearly agreed they had identified the best options. And with the resort's location on Lake Washington, the right solution would carry the development a long way with local environmental groups.

Rolling up the final set of plans, she tucked them into the cardboard tube and laid them next to the others on her drafting table. Everything was ready for Monday. She could take tomorrow off and spend it with Dalton.

A digital bell sounded. Grabbing her bag, she dug through it and retrieved her cell, thumbing to the text message.

Dinner has been moved to 7:00, same location. Marcus.

Glancing at the clock, she realized she wouldn't be able to make it there by seven. Her father abhorred tardiness. By bumping up the dinner plans, he'd made it impossible for her to arrive on time.

"Jackass," she muttered, shoving her cell in her bag and fighting the urge to run for the door. No matter what she did, she was going to be late. He'd set her up to fail, putting her off balance before she even arrived.

Anger surfed the waves of nausea cresting in her stomach. This was so typical of him. He couldn't just *tell* her what he wanted. No, he had to set up a situation where the dinner table became the boardroom and nothing was what it seemed. Every comment would hold innuendo and every response would harbor repercussions.

The garage door slammed behind her, splitting the silence of the vacant parking garage as she stalked to her car, the sharp staccato clip of her heels loud in the low-ceilinged space.

Nothing about tonight held much promise. At least Dalton would be there at the end. Although how they would meet up again was another minefield. Having him come to Bathtub Gin would only invite gossip, and going to the strip club was out of the question.

Maybe she could get him to meet her at her place.... Fingers pressed against her lips, she smiled. All day she'd been trying—and failing—to keep her mind off his kiss, his taste, his tongue. A shiver ran through her and she rubbed her thighs together. *Man, that tongue.* He'd been amazing, the most thorough and attentive lover she'd ever experienced.

And there was more to it than just a one-night, casual fling. He'd held his own with her. He'd been compassionate but not soft, generous but not overbearing. He'd also seen through her, cutting through to the source of her anxiety and making her feel safe. How he'd known what to say, what to do, to alleviate the worry still dumbfounded her. No one, *no one,* read her that well except Gwen, and that had taken years for her friend to perfect.

A soft mist fell, growing dense enough to require intermittent wipers by the time she made it to the restaurant's valet parking. Waiting in line for an attendant, she dug out her small makeup kit, touching up her powder and applying fresh lipstick. It would have to do.

Annoyance stabbed at her temples when she saw Marcus step out the front doors to greet her. Wherever her father was lately, Marcus followed. Tall and decidedly handsome in a cultivated, moneyed way, she had to admit he was easy on the eyes. That didn't mean she wanted to spend her mornings waking up to his face. The sooner he accepted that fact, the better.

Dalton's sleepy grin flashed through her mind. He'd been so sexual and raw, primal even, when he woke up this morning. She bit her bottom lip. Cursing softly, she scrubbed the fresh lipstick off her teeth with one finger.

Marcus said something to the valet supervisor, slipped him a few bills and pointed at her car. The man nodded and started toward her. Several other drivers shifted irritably to see what was going on, who she was to merit immediate attention. One man went so far as to roll his window down and say something sharp to the valet. The young man nodded and replied, but he still skipped the three cars in front of her to help her out of her car before issuing a claim ticket and slipping into the driver's seat.

A firm hand settled on her waist and pulled her into an equally hard body. "You look amazing."

Closing her eyes, she took a moment to center herself. "Please remove your hand from my hip, Marcus."

"You don't need to be so cold, Cass. I'm simply guiding you to the restaurant. I'll take you wherever you want to go," he murmured, infusing his words with suggestive sexuality that crawled over her skin.

"You mean that big building right in front of me, well-lit and overflowing with activity? I'm relatively certain I can find it myself, thanks." Her words were as hot as his response was cold.

"You certainly weren't averse to having a man's hands all over you earlier."

She stepped out of his reach and whipped around to face him. "Excuse me?"

"I saw you with him, you know. The view was great from the lobby." He considered her briefly. "But why would you send a man up the side stairs instead of bringing him through the main entrance with you? Ashamed of him?"

Fury, both at being spied on and at the truth in his statement, made her lash out. "That had nothing to do with you. Learn to take no for an answer already." Wrapped in anger, she spun and started for the restaurant doors.

He kept pace with her. "You came in from the rain, eyes bright and lips swollen. Don't play the objecting female with me, Cassidy." He seemed to pull himself together as he opened the front door and gestured her in. "Your father is waiting. After you."

She nearly leaped away, putting enough distance between them that he couldn't touch her without it being awkward. Heart lodged in her throat, she wanted to run. She wanted to slap him. She wanted to verbally slice him up. Nothing would come together for her, though. All she could do was half walk, half jog to the front doors and slip inside, where Marcus was less likely to touch her again.

The coat check representative took her Burberry and issued yet another claim ticket. Slipping it inside her clutch, she paused in front of the maître d'. "David Jameson's table."

Marcus took her by the elbow and steered her around the podium. "We've already been seated. Right this way, Ms. Jameson."

One more thing to throw me off balance. She let him direct her toward a quiet table in the back, but she yanked her arm free before she slipped into the chair he pulled out for her. Her father didn't bother to rise.

David Jameson picked up his signature bourbon and took a generous sip, considering her over the rim of the glass. "You're late."

She squelched the urge to apologize at the last second. Instead, she ground out, "You made it impossible for me to be otherwise."

"I push you to be better, to anticipate. What you do, or fail to do, is on your shoulders. Not mine."

A thread of hurt wove through the fabric of her emotions, malignantly eating a hole in her self-righteous anger. She clung to that anger, though, refusing to yield. He wanted to goad a response from her, and she wasn't going to give him the satisfaction.

Snapping her napkin out and laying it across her lap before the waiter had a chance, she glared across the table. "You taught me to have broad shoulders."

He paused, highball glass halfway to his lips, and waited.

Cass shrugged. "Broad shoulders were the only way I could ensure I had plenty of room to carry the disappointment you constantly heaped on me."

David Jameson's eyes glittered dangerously.

Bracing herself, she waited.

His gaze shifted when the waiter appeared at her shoulder and asked for her drink order.

"Michelob Light in the bottle," she answered, daring her father with a stare to comment on her "common" drink choice.

He said nothing.

Until the waiter left.

Leaning forward, he set his glass down with the same calculated precision he seemed to do everything. Everything but love her. Forearms on the table, he laced his fingers together. "I understand your little engineering venture received EPA approval for the Chok Resort." A slow blink. "Tell me about your runoff solutions and cost estimates for implementation."

The waiter returned and set her drink down in front of her. He offered to take their dinner orders, but Cass stopped him. "Could you give us a few minutes? I haven't even looked at the menu."

"Of course." With a nod to the men, the waiter left.

Turning her attention back to her father, she forced her hands to remain open and light in her lap. Neither man needed to see the stress winding its way through her. Her father, in particular, would assume he was affecting her. Of course he would. And he'd be right. But she refused to hand him the evidence. *To hell with him.*

"You're asking me to share proprietary information?" She took a slow sip of her beer.

"It's not proprietary. You're family. You have an obligation," he responded so softly she was forced to lean forward to hear him.

"I have an obligation to my *client* to serve his best interests, and it's in his best interest for me to keep that information confidential. I don't owe the family anything." The vehemence with which she delivered that last caught her off guard. She'd never voiced that particular sentiment. Oh, she'd *thought* it, had definitely believed it, but hadn't *said* it.

Her father flattened his hands on the table and leaned forward, his voice containing the hard edge he used to intimidate his opponents. Too bad for him she'd grown up hearing it. "You listen to me, Cassidy Jameson. I received information this morning that the development company has run into funding problems. That means I have the opportunity to seize control of the project. We're talking a seven-figure paycheck here, Cassidy. For the family. I'll make sure enough business is funneled to your little engineering effort you'll have to double staff just to keep up."

She pulled the napkin from her lap, pushing away from the table and standing. Her breath came in short, shallow puffs. "You're offering to pay me for information."

Her father also rose, and Marcus followed suit. "I'm offering to pay you more than the competition to ensure the job goes to the most competent development company. Nothing more."

"No. You're *bribing* me. Color it any way you want, but what you're doing is both unethical and illegal." She dropped her napkin on the table. "I don't work that way, Mr. Jameson, and neither does Preservations."

He arched a brow at her. "Always so naive, even when

faced with irrefutable facts. Your company does, indeed, work that way."

Stomach going into free fall, Cass realized what he was saying—the information about the EPA clearance had come from a mole inside her company. Bile burned her throat and forced her to swallow convulsively. "Not naive, just disappointed, but that sentiment doesn't change my answer. You're not getting the information, not from me or anyone on my payroll." Forcing herself to casually retrieve her claim tickets for her coat and car from her purse, she tucked her handbag under her arm. "Now, if you'll excuse me, I have other obligations."

"Don't walk away from this, Cassidy," Marcus said, his tone low.

"Never think you can tell me what to do." She pushed her chair under the table. "Don't ever come near me again. Either of you." Moving with famed Jameson precision, she turned and strode toward the front of the restaurant, ignoring Marcus's soft demand that she stop.

Her hands shook as she accepted her coat. They shook when she tipped the valet. They shook when she gripped the steering wheel in her car. They were still shaking when she reached Bathtub Gin for the company celebration.

She had a feeling they wouldn't stop until she was in Dalton's arms again.

ERIC CUT HIMSELF SHAVING. Twice. As pissed off as he was, he was lucky he hadn't slit his throat. His brother had finally called him back—on his bus ride home. He'd explained he wasn't eligible to reenroll at school until his tuition was paid via certified funds. Those were funds Eric didn't have.

He nicked himself again.

"Keep this up and you'll go on stage looking like you were shaved by Sweeney Todd," he muttered with the last swipe of his blade.

Dabbing at the nicks and cuts, he cleaned himself up before grabbing a pair of jeans and a rugby shirt, slipping into the pants but tossing the shirt onto the bed. No need to bleed all over the collar.

Cass had a thing at Bathtub Gin tonight. He had to wonder if she'd show up at the club afterward. The thought made him a little ill. There was no shame in doing what he did for a living, but he didn't want her to see him dance on stage or work the floor afterward. It was a far cry from dinner at the Metropolitan. Pacing, he let his mind wander while he waited for the deepest wound to stop bleeding. *What's she doing? What kind of lingerie will she wear today? Is she daydreaming about me? About us?*

The last thought made him laugh out loud. "I'm turning into the stereotypical woman in this relationship." That word, *relationship,* still made his stomach do this lazy roll followed by an impossible twist, as if it was a member of the Mongolian contortionists' troupe.

He'd never been hung up on a woman. Never. Until now. She'd changed him, made him crazy in the best possible way, and he wanted so much more of her and from her. But with two jobs and his brother's future on the line, he couldn't afford the distraction for much longer. They'd agreed to keep it casual, and that's what it had to be.

Leaning on his dresser, he looked in the mirror and snapped, "Focus, man. Focus."

"You in here talking to yourself?"

Eric's chin whipped up to find Blake's reflection in his dresser mirror. His shirtless brother leaned in the doorway, arms crossed over an admirably cut torso. "You've been working out."

Blake arched a brow and snorted. "Well, yeah. How the hell else was I supposed to be able to compete with you?"

Stilling, Eric didn't even blink when he asked, "What are you talking about?" An uncomfortable shrug of Blake's shoulders was all the answer he got, so he pressed. "I mean it, Blake. What are you competing with me for?"

"Whatever. Forget I said anything. It was just a stupid comment." He pushed off the door frame, eyes downcast.

"Stop." The command in Eric's voice was undeniable.

Blake stopped and glanced back over his shoulder, face sullen. "What?"

"Answer me, Blake. You can't throw something like that out there and then just walk away. That shit doesn't fly." He crossed his arms over his chest and spread his feet, lifting his chin just enough so that he was staring down at his little brother. It was his boardroom stance and usually got him what he wanted or where he wanted to go.

"You're always so in charge, in control and stuff. You make big money stripping. Women throw themselves at you every night, so you've got your choice of tail. You've got this gig during the day that stands to make you a boatload of cash, too. It's just…you've got it all together and there I am, sitting in a classroom wondering what the hell I'm going to do with my life. I don't know where to go or what to do, but I look at you and…" He trailed off, eyes wide.

"Seems you've been holding that in for a while. Why don't you finish the thought," Eric encouraged softly. When Blake's wide-eyed stare darted away, Eric relaxed and stuck his hands in his pockets. "And what, Blake?"

"I want what you have." He closed his eyes and sighed. "All of it."

Eric wanted to laugh and scream, hug his brother and shake the shit out of the kid who saw only what Eric wanted him to see. Taking several deep breaths, he focused on Blake. "Look at me, man." Blake hesitated. "I'm not screwing around. Look at me."

He lifted his gaze to Eric's, the compliance almost defiant.

Eric smiled. "You're more like me than you realize." The urge to run his fingers through his hair and mess it up made him fist his hands. Glancing at the clock, he fought not to wince. He was going to be late if this heart-to-heart ran any longer than five minutes, and, in his experience, these things always ran longer. But this was his baby brother. If he had to, he'd talk until the sun came up. Nothing was more important. Cass's image slipped through his mind and startled him, but he shut it down. Taking a deep breath, he said, "Blake, what you see is the superficial stuff."

"That's not true. I know what you've got going on," Blake interjected.

"I didn't say otherwise, did I?" Eric stepped closer to his little brother and felt the chasm of years and responsibilities between them, the two things that made them such different people. Blake still had the option to dream big. Eric had to make it big. Period. A kernel of resentment he'd believed long gone seated itself in his lungs and made his chest uncomfortably tight. Grasping the back of his brother's neck, he gently squeezed. "Blake, I bust my ass, take my clothes off for ones and fives and shake my shit for women four nights a week. It's not glamorous. The work is hard as well as physically and emotionally demanding. These women—" he tried to find the best way to put it "—they want the illusion, not the reality. Don't you get that? They don't want *me*. They want the man they think Dalton Chase is."

His heart nearly stopped. *Isn't that what Cass wants? Isn't that what I've given her?* Hell, he hadn't even offered her his real name.

Shaking his head hard, he huffed out a breath. "I would give anything to have the development company on its feet and making enough that we could survive comfortably off of it, but that may take a while. Hell, it may not ever happen." Dropping his hand, he leaned his forehead against the door casing. "Just…don't envy what you don't completely understand."

"Why didn't you tell me how hard things were?" Blake's quiet question held accusation.

Eric rolled his head to the side to face his brother nearly eye to eye. "Because I wanted you to have the opportunity that was stolen from me when Mom and Dad were killed."

Blake swallowed, then asked the one question Eric didn't want to answer. "What opportunity?"

"The option to choose, man. To choose what you want to be, when and how and where. I want that for you. I want it to be laid out in front of you like a menu so all you have to do is say, '*That*. That's what I want.' Then you go after it."

Blake's mouth thinned. "And what about you? What about what you want? You didn't ask to be my guardian when they died. You didn't ask for the responsibility of seeing me through college and shit."

Eric slowly pushed off the door frame, his chest so tight now he could hardly catch his breath. "No, I didn't ask for those responsibilities, but you're my brother. I want the best for you. Nothing less will do. And I'll do whatever it takes to make sure you get it."

This time Blake met his gaze, sure and steady. "You should have been straight with me about the financial stuff, Eric. There are things I can do to help. This isn't all on you. It's my life we're talking about—I should own at least fifty percent of the responsibility for it."

Eric chuffed out a laugh and shook his head. "Okay. I'll be more transparent with the finances."

"Not just that." Blake didn't look away. "You need to tell me when we're in trouble. When I can help out. I'm twenty-two. I can manage the truth."

"I get that."

"Then trust me with it."

The truth of Blake's statement drove into Eric hard enough he took a step back. Covering, he turned on his heel and went for his shirt.

"Eric?"

"That's fair." Hands unsteady, Eric pulled on his shirt. "Promise me one thing."

"What?"

"Just promise."

"Not until I hear what it is."

Eric glanced over his shoulder, grinning. "You always so skeptical?"

"I grew up with you. I know the shit you used to pull, so yeah, I'm skeptical."

Eric grinned even though it was the last reaction he expected to have. "Don't ever strip."

"No can do, brother."

Eric nearly choked. "I mean it, Blake."

"So do I. I was thinking I'd give it a shot. If I don't like it, I can always do something else, but this is fast money we need."

Eric shrugged into his leather jacket. Taking a deep breath, he faced Blake. "Wait a few days. Let me see if this deal for Sovereign goes through."

"I audition at two tomorrow with Levi."

"You called him already?"

"Woke him up. Guy's a little grumpy in the mornings, huh?"

"Understatement. Okay, just promise me you'll—"

"No promises, Eric," Blake interrupted. "You didn't ask my permission when you started to strip."

"That was a different situation. I don't want you to end up with something on your résumé that keeps you from getting the job you really want."

Blake shrugged. "Maybe I'll really like stripping. Never know."

Eric opened his mouth to reply, then snapped it shut. What could he say? What possible argument could he make to a good-looking twenty-two-year-old kid when he probably *would* enjoy it?

Rolling his shoulders, he grabbed his cell off the dresser and brushed past Blake. "Just remember to wear a condom," he muttered.

"I don't even work there yet."

"I was referring to the audition."

Blake paled.

"Women hang around early to catch the dancers," Eric said, laughing.

"Oh. I thought you meant—"

"Nope. Levi practices heterosexuality like a zealot. He's worshipping some body every night religiously."

Blake grinned. "My kind of job."

Eric shook his head, striding from the room and toward the front door.

Part of him died at the idea of Blake giving up the opportunity to dream big in exchange for the immediate, short-term payoff. Sometimes the bigger dream was worth so much more than the immediate reality—something he needed to keep in mind when it came to this thing with Cass. Yeah, it would be easier for them both if he broke it off tonight.

10

ERIC SLIPPED THROUGH the stage curtain after his last performance, sweaty and exhausted. Grabbing a towel, he wiped his brow and leaned a shoulder against the wall, still trying to figure out how to blow off meeting up with Cass.

"Hey, man. You okay?" Justin, one of his best friends, tagged his shoulder. "You've been off all night."

Eric looked down at the money tucked in his g-string. "I thought I did okay."

"You *always* do okay with the crowd. I meant here, in real life. Need help sorting something out?"

Shaking his head, Eric shoved off the wall. "Maybe later. I need to shower and get out of here."

Justin's eyes narrowed. "If you have somewhere else to be on a Saturday night when the floor's as hot as it is, there's a woman involved."

"So?"

"So you've been nearly celibate for the past four years." Justin took his turn leaning against the wall and blocked Eric's exit. "I want deets."

"Not many to give. I hooked up with the woman who hired me for the private party." Memories of their evening, their morning after, their kitchen island experience filled his mind with vivid images of soft, pale skin, lush hair, long legs...

"Dude, you're smiling." Justin laughed. "She must be something if you're seeing her again."

Eric shrugged, oddly uncomfortable. "She's pretty awesome."

Levi, Eric's other best friend and a club supervisor, stopped in the hallway. "What are you ladies chatting about?"

Eric snorted. "Hair, makeup, cramps—"

"Sex." Justin tipped his head toward Eric. "Our boy here is finally exercising his questionable charm and getting a little recreational somethin'-somethin'."

"Hey." He tagged Justin's shoulder. "It's..." *What? More than that?* Clearing his throat, he rolled his head, stretching the muscles in his neck.

When Eric didn't say anything, Levi's brows rose in surprise. "Like that, is it?"

"No idea what you're talking about," Eric answered, shoving his way past the two men.

Levi's hand closed over his arm, stopping him. "Hey."

"Leave it alone, Levi."

The other man squeezed Eric's arm. "Just wanted to say I'm glad you're having a little fun. Nothing more."

A little fun. He had no idea how to explain that it was more than fun when it wasn't. Couldn't be. And yet he hadn't been able to stop thinking about her all night. Every time a woman touched him, it felt wrong. He hadn't wanted anyone's hands on him but hers, and that freaked him out. Less than twenty-four hours with Cass and he was already hooked on her—and he wasn't sure he was strong enough to break the habit.

Clearing his throat again, he glanced up, lips twitching. "Thanks. Now hands off before I begin to wonder if you're hitting on me."

"You're totally not my type." Levi winked at him and walked off, leaving Eric laughing.

Still leaning against the wall, Justin considered Eric intently.

Steadily meeting the other man's gaze left Eric's skin crawling with self-awareness. "What?"

"What else is going on?"

"It irritates the hell out of me that you're a psychologist. You know that, right?"

Justin rolled his shoulders in a lazy shrug. "Few more months and I'll have the doctor prefix to prove it. Consider this a free consult. What's going on?"

Eric finally nodded and drew a deep breath. "Fine. I talked to Blake today. The university won't allow him to enroll until I pay tuition. He's insisting on getting a job and helping out."

"Sounds like a good plan."

Eric bristled. "Yeah? For whom?"

"Blake's your little brother, but man, he's not a kid anymore. He's twenty-two. You've got to let him make some decisions, live with the consequences."

His stomach somersaulted around in his belly like a Cirque du Soleil performer. "I don't want him making the same mistakes I made." He looked around and, dropping his chin to his chest, ran his hands through his hair. "I don't want him to end up here, but Levi's interviewing him tomorrow. I want better for him," Eric said, his words so soft they were nearly swallowed by the background music and open space and feminine shouts of approval. "I'm fine with this for me, but not for him. He's…" He couldn't finish the sentence.

Justin did. "He's better than this, right?"

Eric's chin snapped up. "Would you want your sisters stripping?"

"Not particularly fond of thinking of them without their clothes, man. In my mind they wear layers and layers of clothes. Just…don't go there." He shuddered.

"It's no different with me and Blake. He thinks this is a glamorous good time, that it's all booze, parties and hot women."

Justin snorted. "It can be."

"But he's almost done with an Ivy League education. This isn't something he needs on his résumé."

"Maybe not, but here's the thing. This isn't about him. It's about *you*. You're terrified the world is going to find out that Beaux Hommes dancer Dalton Chase is actually Eric Reeves, real estate magnate in the making. You're obsessed with keeping the two identities separate because you harbor this intense shame that you strip for a living. That's all you, Eric. It's probably part of the reason you're so conflicted about this woman."

Eric couldn't have been any more incapacitated than if Justin had punched him in the throat. There was no air. "That's not true."

"Oh? So you've told her about Sovereign? Given her your real name? Invited her to the club?"

"No… I can't risk it."

"Risk what? Someone truly appreciating all the things you do?" Clapping Eric on the shoulder, Justin moved toward the stage when the emcee began the buildup for his set. "If you're not sure about this woman, take her to The Countertop. My mother will be able to size her up. Now, if you'll excuse me, I need to go shake my money-maker and earn that wage." Looking over his shoulder, he grinned. "And you need to make a decision."

Eric stared after him as he disappeared, ashamed to

admit that his friend was right. He had been about to push Cass away before she got too close. Then again, she hadn't exactly been eager to invite him into her life, either. But had he given her the chance? Had he tried to get to know her? His brother had asked him to trust him; maybe he should give Cass the same chance. Starting with meeting her at Bathtub Gin.

THE CELEBRATION HAD BEEN a total success, and Cass's employees were having a great time at the bar. A couple of them had been at the bachelorette party last night. She'd smiled benignly and avoided them.

Lingering in the back of her mind was the knowledge someone had betrayed her to her father. Perusing the crowd as casually as possible, she considered each individual. She trusted everyone here. The idea that any one of them could be a potential traitor made her nauseous. It took what had been a night of celebration and made it one of stressful consideration instead.

And she didn't need the extra stress, either. This thing with Dalton that should have been simple fun had suddenly turned complicated.

Her confrontation with him this morning had been minor, but it had left her rattled. He'd walked out afterward, but not in a manner she was used to seeing a man leave. He'd been frustrated but happy, irritated but smiling. How was she supposed to compartmentalize such opposing emotions in one person when she couldn't do it for herself? A deep sigh, laced with frustration and not a little gin, escaped.

She was going to have to call a cab tonight. Drinking hadn't been on the agenda, but there had been toasts and speeches that ranged from hilarious to heartfelt. The group had worked so hard, and she'd lifted a glass whenever anyone else did because they'd looked to her with their words, seeking validation that Preservations, that *they,* were going to make it.

Both were going to be fine. But those speeches and toasts also meant there would be more cabs than just hers tonight. She'd have to talk to Gwen and make sure she helped coordinate that with the bartenders.

Searching the room for her business partner, she wasn't surprised to find her locked in a steamy embrace with her fiancé. A second sigh escaped, this one far deeper, as Cass watched just long enough to feel a bit voyeuristic. Heat scaled her neck to scald her cheeks and leave her hotter than the room warranted.

But watching those two hadn't brought it on. It was the sight of the man who had just stepped inside the bar's wide double doors that left her reeling, her breath coming short.

Dalton Chase.

She sat silent and still as he cased the room. When their gazes locked and he started her way, her palms began to sweat. Her heartbeat grew wilder, more erratic. Background noises faded away until she was hyperaware of him. Only him.

He stopped at the half-moon table in front of her booth. "Thought I remembered you saying you'd be here."

One of her employees, a woman who'd been at the bar last night after the bachelorette party, gave her a thumbs-up and winked.

Cass fought not to cringe. She didn't owe anyone an explanation for what—or whom—she did. But the woman had as much potential as anyone to be her father's mole. That the employee, *her* employee, could relay a very intimate and potentially career-damaging piece of Cass's private life to the ruthless David Jameson galled.

Glancing between him and the woman, her mouth worked silently, the words she wanted to say as well as those she needed to say clogging her throat

Dalton took a deep breath and hooked his thumbs in his jeans pockets. "You don't seem exactly pleased I showed up."

Her gaze came back to Dalton in time to register the tightening at the corners of his eyes and mouth, the sting of her rejection apparent. Guilt soured her stomach. Or maybe it was disappointment—in herself.

She shook her head, the best and only way she could manage to communicate at the moment. Grabbing her gin and juice, she took a huge swallow. Alcohol stung her nose and made her eyes water, but she didn't care. It also cleared her throat.

"I'm just…surprised to see you. I thought you had to work until late," she wheezed, sounding like an old woman with a three-pack-a-day habit.

Body tightening, he watched her closely, clearly choosing his words carefully. "I decided to cut out early."

This was the moment. She'd either make something of what they'd started or blow it all to hell by trying to hide their involvement. Her vision softened. Thoughts of Marcus filled her mind, crowded by her father's demands and revelations, the two weaving through the memories of the evening until it was a tangled mess of misery and self-loathing. She felt her brows draw together and a frown pull at her lips.

"I'll go, Cass. No big deal." He turned for the door, movements robotic, his face a mask of indifference.

"Stay!" she nearly shouted, scrambling from the booth. Several people looked their way. She ignored them. This wasn't about them. Grabbing his arm and tugging, she forced him to first stop and face her.

Expression still neutral, his eyes were empty. "Stay? Would you like me to also sit, maybe roll over?"

The flat words were razor edged and sliced at her. "That's not fair," she managed. "You caught me off guard."

"I figured a visit from your lover would be a welcome surprise." His lips thinned and he visibly paled. "But maybe not." Pulling free of her grasp, he started for the door with more purpose.

"You *are* a welcome surprise." Her soft words stopped him in his tracks, and she was so damned grateful. The Preservations group had quieted, the only intrusion the muted music from the speakers and the clink of glassware behind the bar. Cass knew all her staff's eyes were on them. It didn't matter. Nothing in that moment mattered besides the man she wanted and the hurt she'd caused him. Swallowing hard, Cass did the only thing she could think to do to make it right. "I'm sorry. A surprise visit from—" she hesitated only briefly "—from my lover did catch me off guard, but you know what? I'm glad to see you, Dalton."

Several voices murmured in the background. She ignored them all. Proclaiming what he was to her, calling him by name, was the best she could offer him.

He turned his head to the side, offering her his profile. "You want to get out of here, Cass?"

"Yeah."

"Meet me in the parking lot."

"Give me five minutes."

"Clock starts now." He strode to the door and shoved through it, never pausing, never looking around.

Cass strode to her booth, grabbed her belongings and headed for the bar to make arrangements with the bartenders to line up several cab companies. They assured her they'd close the tab within the hour and, with Gwen's help, start sending people home.

That left her free to do what she needed to do—figure out exactly where Dalton Chase fit in her life.

With a fortifying breath and only slightly gin-hazed mind, she left the bar.

THE UNCHARACTERISTICALLY DRY air stole the breath from her lungs when she stepped outside. But then strong arms pulled her into a tight embrace and firm lips closed over hers with hot insistence. Clearly the passion between them hadn't peaked. Tongues dueled and teeth clashed as their mouths warred for an upper hand no one could possibly gain. Wanting him as fiercely as she did meant she wasn't about to capitulate, to lie back and take his hunger quietly. No, she'd give as well as take in this arena. If last night hadn't taught him that, he wasn't as bright as she'd credited him with being.

He tightened his embrace, annihilating any scrap of distance between their bodies. Demanding hands wound through her hair and tugged the pins out until it fell loose down over her shoulders. He pulled her head back, and his green eyes bored into hers, hot and hungry.

"I missed you," he rasped, his breath condensing on the cold air.

"And here I thought this was you saying goodbye."

His grin exposed deep dimples. "'Goodbye' would be counterproductive to what I have planned for the evening."

Her brows drew together. "Planned?"

"Unless you're tied up." He hesitated. "Not literally, mind you. What I meant was, if you don't have plans, I'd like to take you out."

"It's well after midnight, Dalton."

"I know. I just…" He let her go and stepped back, running his hands through his hair. "I was trying to think of a way to make the evening a little more…special. Maybe I want to get to know you better."

"Know me."

He glanced up, eyes tight. "Yeah."

"I don't get it."

He shoved his hands in his pockets, his shoulders rolling forward. "Not much to 'get,' is there?"

"Depends." She crossed her arms over her chest, suddenly chilled.

He shed his leather jacket and wrapped it around her shoulders before she could protest. "Why is it so hard to believe that I'm interested in you outside of the bedroom?"

"I've never had a one-night stand that stuck around afterward, Dalton." The admission stung and Cass turned away.

"Have you had that many?"

"Well, no, but—"

"Good." Strong arms pulled her in tight, and Cass snuggled in. He breathed deep and kissed the top of her head. "Have you ever been to The Countertop?"

"I'm not exactly sure what that is."

"It's a restaurant. We did your diner for breakfast. I thought we'd do mine for a midnight snack. They make killer pie. Then we can go back to my place and watch a movie."

"A…movie."

"Don't sound so surprised. It can either be a romantic comedy with a dirty ending or a dirty movie with a dirty ending. Your choice."

Laughter bubbled out of her, effervescent and light, and she tipped her face up to his. "You've obviously got sex on the brain, Mr. Chase." Something dark passed through his eyes so quickly she wasn't sure she hadn't imagined it in the semi-lit parking lot. She rested her hand on his cheek. "You okay?"

He wrapped his hand around her wrist and lifted her hand to kiss her palm. "I've got *you* on the brain, Ms. Wheeler. As I said, I want to spend time with you. I'd like to start by buying you a slice of pie before pretending the most innocent thought in my head is snuggling on the sofa. Then? I want to wake up to you again. This isn't a one-night stand anymore."

Her heart tipped even further, dangerously close to crossing the lines that separated lust from like and like from…whatever was on the other side.

THE NOISE LEVEL in the diner was low at one in the morning. Silverware clinked on plates. Voices of third-shift workers rumbled low against the backdrop of country music playing over the jukebox. The sizzle of frying bacon made Eric's mouth water—almost as much as the woman at his side did. Almost, but not quite.

Eric handed her into a booth and slipped in across from her. For a split second, he'd considered sliding in beside her so he could continue touching her, but he'd held out. He didn't want to smother her.

She glanced around, curious. "How'd you find this place?"

"A good friend's mom works here. I've been coming since I was a teenager and sneaking meals at his house whenever I could." He shook his head and smiled. "She never turned me away."

"Why would she?"

Memories of hard times and slim pickings crept up on him. He'd been so lost after his parents died, wandering and reckless and more than a little out of control. Justin's mom, Darcy, had invited him to dinner and given him a home, disrupting his downward spiral with grace and compassion interspersed with tough love. She hadn't missed a beat since. He dropped by the house to visit her as much as to see Justin, who still lived there. No matter how tight things had been, she'd always welcomed him in, even when her family had been forced to ration what little they'd had.

"Dalton?"

Emotion clogged his throat and made it hard to breathe, harder to swallow. He coughed and shook his head. "Just a second." Trying not to scramble from the booth, he rose and went to the counter. His eyes nearly bugged out of his head when Darcy herself walked around the corner.

Her face lit with genuine happiness. "Er—"

"Dalton," he said, low and urgent. "Just for tonight, Darcy. Please."

Eyes narrowing, she looked over her shoulder at the woman he'd left in the booth. "Is there a good reason you're not telling your date your name? Your *first* name?"

He tugged at his collar. "She met me as Dalton, and I don't want to…" He needed tonight to figure out if he could fully trust Cass, if he could share his other life, his *whole* life, with her. The conversation where he told her who he was would have to be handled with care. Having Darcy blurt out his first name to Cass wasn't the intro he was hoping for.

Darcy's shrewd gaze made him feel as if she saw right through him, and that didn't sit well.

"You *are* going to tell her the truth?" Darcy's question hovered far too close to a demand. "No one deserves to be lied to—" she raised both brows "—Dalton."

He hunched his shoulders. "I haven't been anyone other than who I am."

"If that were true, sweetheart, you wouldn't need to *lie* about who you really are." She patted his face and pulled out her order pad. "You want to order now, or should I come to the table?"

"Come meet her."

Darcy tilted her head, considering him. "She must be something."

"She is."

"Okay, then."

Affection swamped him. He leaned over the counter and bussed Darcy's cheek, earning him a surprised laugh and swat with her order pad. "You're cheeky tonight."

"Just..." His eyes widened. He'd started to say "happy." It had been right there, on the tip of his tongue, and he'd almost said it.

Darcy's eyes warmed. She knew. Somehow, she knew. "I'm happy for you, baby. I'll be even happier when you tell her the truth."

"Soon," he promised, backing toward the booth.

Slipping into this seat again, he reached over and touched Cass's clasped hands. "This is my friend's mom. I'd like you to meet her."

Cass's gaze snapped to his. "Okay."

Darcy set water glasses in front of them and smiled, clearly waiting for the introduction.

Eric's mouth was so dry he could have applied for drought-disaster relief from FEMA. He took a sip of water and cleared his throat. "Darcy Maxwell, may I introduce you to Cass Wheeler. Cass, Darcy is one of my closest friends' mother and the best cook anywhere."

Darcy stroked a hand down his head and squeezed his neck.

Affection or warning? He wasn't sure.

"It's nice to meet you, Cass."

"The same, Mrs. Maxwell."

"Oh, no, sweetie. Just Darcy. I haven't been a missus in more than a decade."

Eric caught the dark memories that flitted through Darcy's eyes. The urge to swoop in and protect her was as rampant as it was impossible to satisfy. Darcy wouldn't allow anyone to save her.

Cass's smile was soft, compassionate. "I'm sorry I touched on something painful. Please, forgive me."

Hands tightening in his lap, Eric could only stare. *She saw Darcy's pain, too. Damn observant woman.* And even being a veritable stranger, Cass had found the right words, short and simple, to offer heartfelt condolences.

The older woman touched Cass's shoulder. "Thank you, Cass. The cost of love is sometimes dear, but I'd rather have loved him all those years than never at all."

It was the most Eric had ever heard Darcy say about her husband, and the longing in her voice made his heart hurt.

"That's a lovely sentiment, Darcy. I envy you having memories so wildly precious that even time and heartache can't diminish them."

Darcy squeezed Cass's shoulder and sniffed, grabbing a napkin from the napkin holder to dab at damp eyes. "Look at me. Sixteen years and I still get weepy. It's just…that's the most beautiful, insightful thing anyone has said to me."

"Please, don't cry." Cass grabbed another napkin and passed it to the woman with a genuine smile. "I have highly sympathetic tear ducts as well as a professional reputation for being a coldhearted bitch. The two can't coexist, so please, no tears."

Darcy glanced between him and Cass. "No one who cries for a stranger could be coldhearted, Cass. May the truth of who you are serve you well."

Eric caught the subversive jab and fielded it with as much grace as he could manage. That was, unfortunately, not much. But he'd brought Cass here to get Darcy's opinion of her, and she'd been clear in what she thought of his date. It made him feel better, validated even, in his desire to trust her with the truth. That conversation was for later, though. Now? Now was time for a little fun. "Hungry, Cass? Everything in the bakery tower is one of Darcy's creations, and every one of them is capable of making you commit crimes to get seconds." She laughed, and his breath hung in his chest.

Cass's laughter faded until she was staring at him with quiet reserve.

He reached out and took her hand, lifting it to his lips for a soft kiss. "How do you feel about chocolate crème pie? It's a religious experience."

"I suddenly feel like praying."

He grinned. "Chocolate crème pie for the princess, then." Her hand spasmed in his and he looked at her carefully. "Everything okay?"

"I'm just excited about the pie."

He'd missed something, but he didn't have a freaking clue what it was.

Darcy arched a brow. "Slice or whole pie?"

"Whole pie to go," he said softly. Tonight was going to be a seduction, and damn if he could get his groove on in front of the woman he considered a surrogate mother.

Hunger, the kind Eric wanted to coax to flame, flared in Cass's eyes.

His cell phone rang. Of all the times in the world…

Letting Cass go, he pulled it out and checked the number, recognizing it immediately. "Sorry. This is the day job. Give me a second." Swiping the screen, he answered the call. "Hey, Dan. What have you got going on in the middle of the night, my friend?"

His chief financial officer's voice vibrated with energy. "Thought you'd want to know I've heard the EPA approved the Chok Resort proposal from the environmental engineers."

Eric's stomach went into free fall. "You're freaking kidding me. How the hell did you find out?"

"You know Jason in accounting?"

"Yeah?"

"His sister is dating a guy who works in their surveying department."

"And you trust his information?"

"I had Jason call his sister to confirm. It's bad news, Eric."

The free fall reached terminal velocity. "Don't sugarcoat it."

"I won't. Hell, I *can't*." Dan took a deep breath. "The approval's in, but the engineer's plan is over budget."

"By how much?" Eric choked out.

"I don't have actual figures, only estimates. But it's a million plus."

He wanted to puke. Swallowing the rising bile, he forced himself to relax his grip on the phone. "And you're telling me this in the middle of the night because…"

"Because I just found out and wanted you to know." Dan snorted. "Bullshit. I wanted to share the misery. I have no idea where we're going to get the money, Eric. We're tapped out with the investors and the board isn't going to pony up any more cash. We're screwed if we don't sort this out."

"Keep that between us," Eric said, his voice low and

tight, controlled. "You don't repeat that to anyone. Jameson will be stalking around like the damned jackal he is, waiting for a chance to steal this project. I need this deal, Dan. *We* need this deal. If we don't get the funding, we're—"

"Dalton?" Darcy's hand rested on his arm. "You okay, sweetie?"

He glanced over. "I'm good."

"Did she just call you Dalton?" Dan asked.

Panic slammed into him, forcing him to dig for yet another lie. "Good friend of the family. She calls me by my middle name when I'm in trouble. We'll discuss this first thing Monday morning. Thanks for the heads-up."

Disconnecting, he turned back to the table to find Cass watching him, brows drawn. He sat down across from her and, hand shaking slightly, took a sip of water. "Sorry about that."

"Is everything okay?"

"Major setback with the day job. It's all going to work itself out."

"Must be major for you to take a call in the middle of the night. What do you do during the day?"

Eric paused before setting his water glass down gently. Time to put his money where his mouth was. "I'm an entrepreneur. I've got a business I'm trying to get off the ground. There's a project I've bid on. Seems I've won the bid and the right to move ahead, but there are complications we'd hoped to avoid. Dan, the guy who called, is my CFO. He thought I needed to know sooner rather than later that the meeting we've got later this week is going to be a bitch."

"You have dedicated employees if they're working in the middle of the night."

"Yeah. I'm lucky." *Or not.* Not if he considered the

money he had to secure to keep the business afloat. He swallowed convulsively.

"Do you have to go handle whatever it is?"

His head snapped up. "No. There's nothing I can do until Monday. Tonight is about us."

"Us, huh? What are we then, Dalton?"

"We're potential with an unknown variable thrown in for excitement."

"I love unknown variables."

"Handy, that. So do I." He shifted and laced their fingers together, the move so natural he wasn't sure what to make of it. Her skin was petal soft. The way her hair hung loose and full made him want to bury his hands in it and kiss her again. He knew what her skin tasted like beneath the fit and finish she presented the world, and he wanted that taste on his tongue again, all feminine and soft.

"Let me box that pie up," Darcy murmured, moving away from the table.

Heat burned across Cass's cheeks. "Why do I get the impression that you're undressing me in your mind?"

He nipped her knuckles. "Because I am."

Her hand twitched then settled. "Fair enough."

"How's that fair?" His grin was immediate as the pieces fell into place. "Unless you're doing the same."

"Give the man a prize…or pie," she whispered, voice as sultry as sex-fueled sin.

Lust punched a wrecking ball–size hole through his thin veneer of control. He leaned forward to take her mouth.

Darcy slid the pie box between them. "On the house."

Eric collapsed in his seat and pulled out his wallet.

"That means 'free,' sweetheart," Darcy insisted.

"I get the concept, but there's still the matter of your tip." He dropped a twenty on the table. "Thanks, Mama D."

"You don't go dropping a twenty for two glasses of water and a few words of conversation," she said primly. "Take that money and go on."

"You can pick it up or not, but I'm leaving it." When she opened her mouth to argue, he stood. "Darcy."

"Oh, you're a stubborn child." She snatched the twenty and shoved it in her apron pocket. "You'll come over for dinner?"

"Soon," he promised, picking up the pie box and offering Cass a hand.

"This week." Darcy pulled him into a fierce hug that defied her tiny stature.

"This week, then."

She winked. "Enjoy the pie." Spinning on her heel, she snatched the coffeepot off the counter burner and moved to a nearby table, chatting up the diners as she went.

"She's a remarkable woman."

Eric looked down at Cass. "She is. I tend to be drawn to them."

"Flattery will get you everywhere."

"There's only one place I want to be."

She glanced up at him through thick lashes. "And where's that?"

"With you, behind closed doors."

"Apparently I'm your genie in a bottle because I can grant that wish."

If Eric had any delusions that his grin was anything other than wicked, the hunger on her face would have dispelled it.

She shrugged into her jacket and took the pie while he did the same.

He moved in close and framed her face with his hands. Closing the distance, he kissed her, long and slow.

She responded with a sigh, opening to him and trying to move closer despite the pie box.

He broke the kiss and, stroking a thumb over her kiss-swollen lips, worked to control his breathing. He may not have given her his real name, but he had made an effort to bring his two worlds together, and she'd fit into both of them. Maybe there was something to this trust thing. "Lucky me."

"Why's that?"

"I've still got two more wishes."

11

THE TRIP TO DALTON'S house was relatively quiet. It wasn't an uncomfortable quiet, but rather a companionable silence that left Cass relaxed and slightly cathartic despite the sexually charged atmosphere. Dalton's presence provided comfort after the stress of the dinner with her father and the situation with the leak from inside Preservations. She wanted to curl up with Dalton and let him hold her. They'd get to that, she was sure—after the movie he'd promised. And pie. Glancing down at the crème-covered delicacy, her stomach rumbled.

Dalton glanced at her and smiled. "I'm going to take a wild guess and say you're hungry."

She turned to stare out the passenger window of her car. The world passed by, sleeping households full of strangers who couldn't care less that she'd had a shitty night. They had their own lives to wrangle. Then there was Dalton. Confusing, alluring, challenging Dalton. He'd given her another piece to the Dalton puzzle tonight, and he'd want more of her in return. But could she give it to him?

He rested a hand on her thigh, her dress having ridden up to expose the bare skin. "Cass? Did you eat tonight?"

Shaking her head, she glanced at him. "No."

"Why not? I thought you were having dinner with your father."

The snort that escaped her was anything but lady-like. "I was invited to dinner. That doesn't mean I was invited to eat."

His brow furrowed as he pulled his hand away to shift gears, navigating a series of residential twists and turns. "I don't get it. Dinner usually implies eating."

"You'd think." Letting her head fall back against the headrest, she closed her eyes. "Dinner with my family isn't ever simple. The appetizer is typically snark with a side of sarcasm, the main course is always parental disappointment seasoned liberally with guilt, and dessert is never complete without a full serving of derision."

"I'm probably going to hate myself for asking this, but how did you end up so amazingly balanced and, well, normal?"

"It was the biggest 'screw you' I could deliver to my parents."

"Ah, the equivalent of the after-dinner mint."

Shocked, she turned to face him and laughed out loud at the benign look on his face. "I'll have to remember that."

His full lips tipped up at the corners as they passed under a series of streetlights, the effect almost strobelike. "Yeah, well, I'm famous for my witty repartee." He ran a hand through his hair, shooting her a quick glance. "Did anyone else show up for the un-dinner?"

"There was a former… Hmm." Biting her bottom lip, she tried to decide how much to say—again. She wasn't sure she wanted to tell him about the confrontation with Marcus because he had scared her, and fear was just another weakness. But Dalton wasn't someone she was facing across a boardroom. He was someone she was fast relying on for comfort and understanding. One of a very few. She shifted onto her hip and faced the man who was fast stealing her heart. "Yes, there was. Remember the roses? The guy who sent them was there. We've been on a couple of dates, but that's all. He's made it clear he'd be interested in more—much more. I'm not. He met me outside and got a little aggressive about us. Me and you, that is."

She braced against the driver's seat as Dalton whipped the wheel to the right and slid the car to a stop alongside the curb.

"Aggressive *how,* Cass?" He stared straight ahead, the knot of muscle at the back of his jaw flexing as he ground his teeth.

Settling her hands in her lap, she fought to control her voice. "It's not important. I handled it."

Even in the unearthly streetlight, she could see him pale. "Did he hurt you?"

"Hurt me?"

"Did he *hurt* you?" He looked at her then, his eyes nearly luminescent.

"No. No, he didn't assault me, Dalton." She rested a hand on his rock-hard jaw and searched his face, this man who had nominated himself as her knight errant. "He just… He scared me, Dalton."

Gently picking up her hands, he turned them over in his own. "He had no right to touch you without your permission. And you don't ever have to face him alone again."

"Who said chivalry is dead?" she whispered, the words loud in the silence of the car.

"It might make me old-school, but I don't think it should be." He shifted the car back into gear and pulled away from the curb.

THEY PULLED UP in front of a small but neat clapboard house, its color indiscernible in the dark. Gray, maybe? Or a light blue with darker trim? Regardless, the yard was neat, the landscaping well tended and the detached, single-car garage was in equally respectable shape.

Dalton parked in the drive and pulled her into a short, brutal kiss.

She gasped into his mouth, their breath comingling as they seemed to fight toward what they both wanted: each other. Fully. Completely. Without physical barriers or pitfalls. Just the two of them. Together. Tonight.

Pulling back, she searched his face for some reassurance. Yes, all the signals he'd sent said that he wanted more from her than just tonight. But how much more? She'd already revealed more than one weakness to him and risked her career. What was *he* willing to risk?

In her experience men were never honest about who they were and what they wanted. Every single man she'd been involved with in any way, from her contentious relationship with her father to her last romantic relationship, expected her to give up every shred of who she was, while they kept themselves at a safe distance and protected their interests. While she fell under that header for them, all was well and good. The moment their interest waned, she was on her own again. She didn't *want* Dalton to follow that pattern. Something in her said that if anyone could be different, it was him. But to give him more? Would he…*could* he even like the parts of herself she kept hidden?

He seemed to interpret her needs, kissing her gently, passion ready to flash at any moment, but he kept it banked. This kiss was different. This kiss made promises far more personal than all the others combined. He loved her with his mouth and hands, caressing her face, sucking on her bottom lip, cupping one breast and stroking her nipple through the silk of her dress.

He broke the kiss but didn't move away, his lips grazing hers when he spoke. "I want you, Cass."

"The feeling's mutual."

He considered her for a moment. "But?"

It disturbed her he could tell so easily that something was bothering her. "I'm worried this is happening too fast."

"I was, too. Until tonight."

Her brows drew together. "What changed?"

"You stood up in front of your coworkers and called me your lover. And I realized no one else matters. I want you. I think you want me, too. We don't owe anyone an apology for following this path."

"Please, don't hurt me." The words were out before she could stop them.

"I'll never hurt you, baby."

An electric jolt of awareness nearly made her hair stand on end. "Don't make promises you can't keep."

"I don't." He closed the distance and took her mouth in a kiss so tender she melted into his embrace.

Eric led Cass into his small house by the hand and wondered, for the first time ever, what a woman thought as she entered. The house needed to be renovated. Badly. But it was homey, with its little nooks and crannies and cupboards built in. The three rooms and two bathrooms were on the small side, but they served their purposes well.

"I love it," Cass breathed, pulling free of him to go examine his mother's beloved china in the built-in cupboard. She placed her fingertip against the wood and traced the grain before opening the door. "May I?"

"Sure."

She carefully removed a teacup. The gentle way she handled the china said she knew it was a cared-for family heirloom and she would respect that.

Examining the old dishes seemed to make her happy, and that made Eric glad he hadn't gotten rid of the china when he'd purged his parents' belongings with some pretty extreme prejudice. Living alone, he hadn't seen the need to keep most of their stuff save for a few mementos. But that china had been his mother's pride, handed down from her great-grandmother, and the thought of getting rid of it had felt like severing the final tie with his mom. He just couldn't.

Blake had been pretty good about helping clean things out the first summer he'd been home from college.

College. Eric's mind seized on the reminder that he had to cover yet another semester's costs. Coming up with the funds was going to financially destroy him if this resort deal didn't go through. Now that the engineering firm's costs were going to come in over budget, the financing would be even more precarious. Wednesday morning weighed on him as he absently watched Cass admire a painting his grandmother had done. *This has to work.* He jolted, unsure what he'd been referring to—the deal or the woman.

Both, his conscience whispered.

He stepped toward Cass, fighting to regain control of his runaway thoughts. But it was like trying to harness shadows. He stopped short and silently watched as Cass moved on from the dishes to first one antique piece then another, appreciating the very things his mother had held so dear. Long, capable fingers skimmed timeworn surfaces with such tenderness he wanted to scoop her up and simply hold her in his arms.

So he did.

Her body molded to his as if they'd been cast as a matching pair. *Stop thinking this way, dumbass,* he mentally chastised. It would only lead to problems if this didn't...what? What was he looking for from her? Definitely something more than a weekend fling or short, fiery love affair.

She was exactly the kind of woman who could inspire him to crave constancy, the kind of woman he could see himself settling down with someday. He wanted to find out where this thing between them would go, how far they could take it, and he'd never been interested in the same with anyone else. He wanted Cass in his bed, in his house, in his life far more permanently than just a weekend love affair. She deserved better than that. Which meant she also deserved the truth.

She stepped out of her heels and toed them against the wall. "May I ask exactly what happened to your parents? I know you lost them several years ago." Moving to the mantel, she traced the edge of a framed picture of him and his little brother fishing at a lake they used to take camping trips to every summer.

His stomach knotted so fast he nearly doubled over with pain. Normally he handled the devastating subject by deflecting. He'd change the topic or talk about the Mariners' miserable season or, hell, discuss the local forecast. But she'd looked at him with such open compassion that he wanted to tell her about the gaping wound their loss had left in his life.

The emotional dam that held so much at bay failed, and the words rushed out. "They were killed fourteen ago when a logging truck's brakes failed coming down Snoqualmie Pass. The driver...he..." Eric swallowed hard and sank to the sofa, the heels of his hands pressed against his eyes. He didn't talk about this. Ever. Yet here he was, answering her without evasion.

A warm hand closed over the back of his neck. "That's more than enough."

He nodded, unable to speak. At that moment, he would have given anything to have his parents alive again, would have loved to introduce them to this woman who, once again, understood exactly what to say in the face of emotional devastation.

"You really did raise your little brother. I admire that."

Eric coughed and cleared his throat, dropping his hands to stare at the floor. Bare feet with toenails painted a deep blue came into focus, and he found himself relaxing. "He was nine years old."

"You helped shape him into the man he's going to be. Don't discount that. It couldn't have been easy." She stroked his hand.

He pulled her close and wrapped his arms around her waist. Resting his head against her breasts, he relaxed as her deft fingers massaged his scalp. His eyes drifted closed and his breathing slowed, and suddenly it was just okay. Not okay that his parents had died, but okay that he'd talked to her, okay that he'd been less than stalwart about it. Just okay. It was the greatest gift she could have given him, and he didn't know how to say thank you. Instead, he looked up to find her dark blue eyes staring back with somber compassion.

He ran a hand up and down her spine. "How about that movie?"

"Sure." Bending so their faces were level, she kissed him incredibly gently. "But I really want out of this dress."

His breath caught.

She laughed. "If you have a T-shirt and boxers I could borrow, I'd be really grateful."

"They'll swallow you whole, but yeah. Let me grab them." He stood and was moved when she slipped her arms around his waist. "What's this?"

"I've heard it called a hug," she murmured into his chest.

"Smart-ass," he said into her hair as he wrapped his arms around her shoulders and held her tight. He was struck again by how right she felt here, not only here in his arms but here in his house and, if he was honest, in his life. It was a bit of a daunting realization, but he wasn't surprised. Not after watching her with Darcy, amazed by how she had a sense for just what to say and when. More, that she meant it. Everything about her was almost too good to be true. "When is the other shoe going to drop?"

She tilted her face up to meet his gaze. "Other shoe?"

"You know. When are you going to tell me you're actually married, or that you're wanted by the FBI because you hacked into KFC and stole the Colonel's secret recipe for the Russians, or that you've been entered into the witness protection program because you single-handedly brought down the Italian mafia, or that you're actually the droid I've been looking for?"

She was laughing at that point. "What in the world are you talking about?"

Cupping her neck, he traced his thumbs back and forth along her pulse. "You're too good to be true, Cass. I keep waiting for you to screw up, but you handle everything that's thrown at you with this unerring grace and infallible strength. You're pretty amazing."

Her laughter faded until they were staring at each other in a room whose only sounds were those of an old house—the click of the furnace, the whoosh of air through the central heating system, the drip of a faucet somewhere nearby, the quiet hum of the refrigerator.

"I'm just me, Dalton."

He fought not to wince. In this moment, a moment that meant something larger than he could wrap his mind and heart around, he didn't want her calling him by his middle name.

He wanted to hear her call him Eric. He was going to tell her—tonight.

He was all-in.

12

CASS HAD NO IDEA what movie Dalton put in and would bet good money he didn't know, either. Before the previews were over, they were lost to each other. Tender but passionate, he laid her down on the beige sofa and began to kiss his way down her neck. He peeled her dress off as he went. The sofa's pilled, coarse fabric scraped at her back, but she didn't care. It was the moment, this moment, the reality of his hands on her body and the feel of his silken lips roaming bare skin that mattered. She touched as much as she was touched, tasted as much as she was tasted. Cravings for Dalton had morphed into a need so fierce she was helpless to deny it. That need drove her, made her clumsy and rushed, pushing Dalton's own passions higher and hotter until he was devouring her and finally, finally she had the fervor and near madness she hungered for.

They slipped to the floor with a muffled thump when he tried to roll her over on the sofa. His head cracked against the hardwood floor with its own thump, she on top of him. But that didn't slow him down. His hands roved over her, his thumbs thrummed her nipples through her bra and her sex ached as she mindlessly ground against the ridge of his erection through his jeans. She closed her hands over his on her breasts and rode him harder, the friction from the satin and denim against her clit, the hard line of his cock and her desire culminating in an explosive orgasm that had her crying out his name and squeezing her hands over his.

"Cass." Dalton's sharp voice cut through the haze of her lust and forced her to focus on him. Muscles strained in his neck, his face was flushed and he looked as if he was trying desperately not to...

"Oh. Sorry." She started to move off his lap, but he refused to let go of her breasts.

"Just sit still for a second so I don't embarrass myself." He closed his eyes and breathed, hands gradually relaxing their hold. When he finally looked at her, the corners of his eyes wrinkled with a sheepish grin. "I haven't nearly lost control like that since I was a teenager."

"I hear age does that to a man."

"Age?" He flipped her over, cradling her head so it wouldn't hit the floor. "I'll show you age."

She arched a brow. "Surely not before you admire the lingerie."

"Lingerie." He gazed down and traced a finger across the swell of one breast where black lace and pale skin met. "I want to see you in this, the thong and the heels. Nothing else."

Pushing herself up on her elbows, she pressed her lips to his in what was meant to be a quick kiss but evolved into a long, drawn-out affair that left her squirming and him panting and a repeat performance on the horizon.

"For the love of all that's holy, Cass, save my pride. I can't hold out again."

Her breathy laugh was all the answer she could muster.

He rolled off her and hooked an arm behind his head, jerking his chin toward her shoes.

"I'll let you boss me around right now because I'm one up in the orgasm count, but don't think it'll become a regular habit," she teased, clutching her dress and standing.

"I wouldn't mind it becoming a regular habit," he said softly.

She faced him, brow furrowed. "Please don't tell me you get off ordering me around. That could be a problem."

"No, baby."

Something in her bloomed at the pet name.

"I meant I could get used to this, us, being a regular thing."

Yep. Definitely bloomed. The urge to run to him, to buy into the mystery and security and promise of a happily-ever-after nearly overwhelmed her. Instead of giving in to the urge, she moved toward her shoes. She wasn't that girl.

Her father had changed her worldview as a young girl when he'd strolled through the media room while she'd been watching *Beauty and the Beast*. He'd paused and then burst out laughing when Beast transformed into a handsome prince. Once he'd regained his breath, he'd told her the concept of true love was as much a lie as Santa Claus, and that relationships were about economics, even to princes. She hadn't known Santa was a lie, and the truth had left her in tears.

"Oh, grow up," he'd barked before yelling for her nanny, Paulette, and slamming the door behind him.

Paulette had consoled her. She'd also confirmed that Santa wasn't real, leaving Cass to draw the only conclusion a seven-year-old girl could draw: if Santa was a lie based on money, love must also be a lie based on money. Successive boyfriends hadn't changed her opinion.

"Cass?" A warm hand caressed her calf and she jumped out of reach. "Hey." Dalton rose and moved in behind her. "Where'd you go?"

"An unhappy stroll down memory lane," she whispered.

"If memory lane is full of unhappy memories, let's make some happy ones of our own."

She glanced over her shoulder, unable to mask the surprise on her face. "What do you mean?"

"Don't look so scared." He stroked her hair off her forehead. "I'm not asking for a declaration of undying love. I'd just like to see where this goes, try and make it work." He swallowed. "Maybe get to the point of exclusivity."

"I don't sleep around, Dalton." Her words came out harsher than she intended. "Sorry. It's just… I don't date a lot and if I'm sleeping with someone, I don't go out with anyone else. It feels wrong."

He nodded. "Cheapens the experience of what you have with the person you're sleeping with."

She relaxed a little. "Exactly."

"You know what this means?"

"No?"

Pushing himself into a sitting position, he winced and rearranged his erection so it wasn't pinched in his jeans. "It means we've crossed the first bridge."

Her stomach did a weird tumble through her and paused somewhere near her knees. "Which bridge?" His answer made her stomach finish the fall.

"We've just become exclusive."

She rubbed a hand over her thundering heart and fought for air. "Exclusive" hadn't been on the menu when she'd met Dalton *yesterday*. "Don't you think it's a little fast for that?"

"Not really." He pierced her with a bold green stare. "We just established we're not sleeping with other people. I'm not seeing anyone else while I'm with you because I really don't want to. You said you don't date much, so I'm going to assume you're not seeing anyone else, either." He frowned, his gaze becoming fierce. "Unless we're talking about Marcus, and then I'll have to kill the slimy son of a bitch."

A nervous half gasp, half laugh escaped before she answered. "No, I'm not dating Marcus."

He grinned at her. "Then you just saved his life."

"You scare me a little," she said, the words a whisper.

His brows winged down. "You realize I'm joking, right? I'm not some super-secret government agent spy guy here to bring down the dastardly Marcus for moving on my woman, right?"

"Your woman." That was all that she'd heard. One part of her was ecstatic she could have this man completely to herself, but the other part of her was terrified.

His face relaxed and did that neutral thing he did when he was trying to hide how he felt. "You don't look happy."

Already she didn't like watching him try to hide what was real. She took a deep breath and slipped on the heels, then she slowly turned and faced him. The urge to cover herself made her hands twitch, and she fought to stand there and let him stare as she spoke. "I don't wear matching lingerie and stilettos for just anyone, Dalton."

"But that doesn't mean you're happy," he replied, face still carefully blank.

But his eyes—oh, man, his eyes. They had darkened with a riot of emotion and watched her now with such base desire she shivered.

"I'm happy," she assured him as she did her very best, very slow catwalk stalk toward him. "Very, very happy."

"Then why did you hesitate?"

Clearly he wasn't going to let this go so she stopped, closing her eyes before answering him. "Because I suck at relationships. I don't believe in happily ever after. I've fought long and hard to carve out my place in the world, and it's never included anyone with any type of longevity except Gwen. With her, it's like I'm a ship and she's a barnacle," she said with a soft smile. "A tiny, tenacious, terrifying barnacle who didn't give me the option to say no and loves me in spite of myself."

The rustle of fabric and creak of floorboards made her open her eyes—she fully expected to find Dalton leaving the room. Instead, she found him closing the insignificant distance between them. "What kind of ship?"

"Huh?"

He smiled slowly. "What kind of ship are you? I'm thinking pirate ship."

She laughed. "I'm a pirate ship?"

He pulled her into a fierce hug that completely enveloped her. He settled his mouth beside her ear, and his words were little more than an exhale. "Yep. Know how I can tell?"

"How?" she asked, just as softly.

He nibbled his way down her jaw and across to her mouth, his lips moving over hers when he answered. "I have a real thing for pirate ships. Must be the booty." Swift and sure, his lips pressed to hers and demanded she answer in kind. It was a kiss that moved her and stilled her, freed her and branded her. And that's when Cass knew. She was in trouble. *Big* trouble. The kind of trouble a heart didn't want to be rid of. Ever.

He lowered her to the floor as he whispered into her ear what he was going to do to her body.

She went willingly and with the full understanding that what happened tonight was another step toward the impossible.

For once, she tuned it all out and let herself fall into Dalton.

THE SMELL OF COFFEE drifted through Eric's consciousness. He stretched, groaning. Memories of last night rolled through his mind as his synapses began to fire. Man, it had been wild. *Cass* had been wild. She'd been tentative, at first gun-shy of the idea they were actually going to try exclusivity. Then something in her had shifted. Every presumption he'd had vanished in that vixen's wake. He'd never been owned in the bedroom, but she'd managed it in the very best ways possible. So efficiently, in fact, he was physically sore. He grinned. Each aching muscle was like a badge of freaking honor. He'd *earned* them and would damn straight do it all over again given the opportunity. Maybe even tonight.

He was a little uneasy that he still hadn't broached the subject of his name, but she'd been so vulnerable last night, he hadn't wanted to risk hurting her. Besides, they still had today, and he'd spend it making her so happy she wouldn't care what his name was.

"What has you lying there, eyes closed, looking like the guy who knows he won the lottery the day after he signed the divorce papers?"

He opened his eyes, slow and lazy. "You."

"Uh-uh." She sipped her coffee. "I wasn't even in here."

"I was doing a little play-by-play recap. I'm pretty

sure we both scored repeatedly, but I'm not sure who won the game."

She patted his cheek. "Silly man, I did."

"How can you be sure?" Skepticism wove through his words.

"Because you're the player, baby, but I'm the coach."

"Put your coffee down."

"What?" Her gaze slid to him, and he was totally charmed at the way her lips twitched and her eyes shone.

"I said put your coffee down."

"Why?" Now the skepticism was all hers.

"I don't want you to spill it and burn yourself."

She snorted. "I think I can manage to hold a conversation and sip a cup of coffee without burning myself."

He arched a single brow. "You won't be able to when I take you to the mat...Coach." She was off the bed in a flash, her alarmed squeak making him laugh. "What kind of coach runs from her players?"

"The kind who knows the size of bat her player swings." Scarlet stained her cheeks. "I'm a little sore."

"No batting practice this morning," he said gently and patted the bed. "Have a seat."

"Okay, but hands under the covers and you keep them to yourself." Her eyes flared and her mouth opened and closed as he roared with laughter. "I didn't mean... That is... Well, shit." She chuckled, shaking her head.

"So no batting practice, huh?"

She grinned. "Shut up, Dalton, or you'll be benched indefinitely."

"Shutting up immediately, Coach."

"Good," she said demurely, settling on the bed and tucking her legs up under her. "What are your plans for the day?"

The question caught him off guard, and he blurted the

truth out without an ounce of finesse. "I thought we'd spend it together."

Her mouth quirked to one side as she considered him. "I really should go into the office. I've got a big meeting—"

Sitting up, he took her coffee cup from her, sipped and grimaced as he set the cup on the nightstand. "I know you said you like it with cream and sugar, but there's enough crap in there to disqualify this as coffee."

"Men who bitch rarely get their own cup," she teased, hopping up and grabbing a second mug he hadn't noticed off the chest of drawers. "The three *b*'s—basic, black and bitter. Just the way you like it."

The only way she could have known how he took his coffee was if she'd taken note of how he'd made it yesterday at breakfast. And she would have only taken note if she'd wanted to bring it to him today, and maybe tomorrow and the next day and… His heart stuttered. This woman could be so much trouble for him. Trouble with a capital *L* for…

He choked on the hot brew and sat up, spitting coffee everywhere.

"Dalton?" She grabbed a pillow, ripped the case off and began dabbing at the coffee-stained comforter. "Either give me the international sign for choking or a thumbs-up that you're ready to die."

"Don't make me laugh," he wheezed. Wiping at his tearing eyes, he watched her with a kind of terrified curiosity.

She whipped her hands back, tucking the pillowcase behind her. "Sorry about the pillowcase, but I didn't want you to ruin your comforter. It's cheaper to replace sheets than a comforter set."

Cold reality crept into the moment and flash-froze his

lungs. It always came down to money with him. *She realizes I need the cash.* Nerves rattling along his spine like an inmate raking an empty tin cup against metal bars, Eric watched her silently until her brows winged down.

"What?"

"Why did you suggest that sheets were more reasonable to replace?" He hated that his voice reflected the frigid wasteland of resentment spreading through him. Had he been deceiving himself to think that she would accept him, poor stripper that she thought him to be? "Cass?" he pressed.

"A part of me can't justify throwing out a comforter for a minor stain. Sheets are easier and cheaper to replace if the coffee stain doesn't come out." She glanced at him again, her jaw set in a stubborn line. "I might live in a nice apartment, but that doesn't automatically make me irresponsible with my money."

He fought to keep his jaw from dropping. She thought... "So that —what you just said—isn't about me at all." He couldn't help but push her for clarification.

"If you believe I'm a spendthrift, you've got me wrong entirely. I—"

Relieved, he cut her off midsentence, his mouth crashing down onto hers. His tongue danced across hers, seductive and demanding, as he slid his hands up her arms to cup her neck. Lacing his fingers together so he held her immobile, he took the kiss deeper. She tasted of sugared coffee and toothpaste and of something inherently *her*. That half-crazy craving she fueled spun up inside him. His hands involuntarily tightened on her neck.

She whimpered.

Had he been a true gentleman, he would have let her go. Instead, he tightened his hands again, his fingertips curling to press firmly into her skin. His cock kicked and his testicles drew up close to his body. After last night, he was almost spent, but he wasn't dead. Dry brush burned when it tried to embrace a live flame, and she was the fuel to his tinder.

Without warning, she pulled away, eyes wide and lips swollen. "What the hell was that, Dalton?"

Dalton. Never Eric. That's going to change. Today. "My way of asking you to stay."

"And actual words wouldn't have worked?"

"I was reminding you why you should stay, reminding you that what's between us isn't your average, run-of-the-mill, flash-and-burn attraction and you shouldn't use your work to hide from it."

Silent, she stared at him.

He stared back, watching as she worked through whatever it was she needed to in order to stay here with a clear conscience. Had he said too much? She was so unyielding, watching him without a word, that he feared he'd snap, throw her over his shoulder and carry her back to bed in an effort to convince her to not to leave. They always connected between the sheets. If that's what it took to get her to realize they were great together then—

"Don't order me around, Dalton. I don't like it."

His laugh was part shock, part humor given what he'd just been considering. Still, he managed to sort out his thoughts. "I'll work on it. I don't want you threatening to run every time I slip, and I *will* slip, Cass. I'm human and I'm male, and those two things apparently mean I'm going to screw up on epic levels time and again."

One corner of her mouth curled up, but her eyes remained still and deep. "I can handle you screwing up if you're truly trying, but the demanding and commanding crap? It doesn't work. It pushes every defensive button I have and it will send me through your front door so fast the only thing I'll leave behind is the cartoonlike outline of me as I exit."

Clearly she was still jumpy as hell. He'd need every minute of the next twenty-four hours if he had any hope of reassuring her he wasn't playing her once he'd told her the whole truth.

"Spend the day with me, then stay tonight. Let's get out of here and have a play date."

This time her grin reached her eyes. "Play date?"

"It'll be fun. Trust me." He reached for her hand, and she reached back.

"Okay."

"Okay what?"

"Okay, I'll stay today and spend the night. But I do have to get up at the butt crack of dawn and be at work around six. Are you cool with that?"

"Yep. I've got a metric shit-ton of stuff to do tomorrow, too, so that works out. We can meet for lunch, maybe grab a burger, sneak a few kisses and wrap up the day with me making you an amazing dinner."

"Don't make too many plans."

"Why not?"

"Nothing good ever lasts for me, Dalton, and this feels way too good."

The language was simple, the words direct. The hell of it, though?

She was right.

13

CASS WAS ALWAYS on time. She liked schedules. She did well with agendas and plans and structure. Today, though, there were so many stops and starts, usually involving tender kisses and less-than-innocent touches, that it took them forever to get out of the house. She couldn't have cared less. Every touch made it worth the hours it took them to get to her car and head toward the waterfront. He was so far away from her regular world, she didn't even think about Preservations or the mole or the big meeting in just a few days.

He'd quickly passed with a gruff, "No thanks," when she offered to take him back to Bathtub Gin to pick up his car. Pressing had seemed silly, but part of her was suddenly curious about what the kind of car he drove. It didn't matter to her one bit, but it clearly mattered to him. The realization made her want to push the issue, to find out what bothered him about his car. It was obvious he was cautious with money. Was it because he had to be? Did he get the impression money mattered to her? Did he think she lived large? Was it her address? Was it that he was ashamed of some facet of how he lived or what he did?

Sort of like you struggling with his occupation, maybe? her conscience whispered.

Frowning, she rubbed her forehead. It wasn't that. It *wasn't.*

Warm fingers traced down the side of her cheek and reclaimed her attention. "What's with the dark scowl?" he asked from the passenger side.

She shrugged, glancing at him before returning her attention to the road. "Nothing. It's fine."

Wrapping his hand around the far side of her headrest, he leaned toward her.

She started hard enough she actually jerked the wheel.

"Right. Clearly you're not bothered at all."

The teasing in his voice made her relax a little. "I have to concentrate. I didn't grow up running around Seattle like some wild child."

"I resent the implication that I was a wild child."

"And why is that?" she absently asked, looking over her shoulder as she merged into traffic on I-5.

"I'm not so old I can't still be a little wild," he answered, running a hand up the inside of her near thigh.

"You've got that right."

"Recognize the reality, woman."

"What I 'recognize' is that you're going to make me wreck the car if you don't get your hands off me."

"Decrepit, but I've still got it."

His answer, and fingertips, surprised a laugh from her. "And modest with it, too."

"Why pretend modesty when it's clear I speak naught but the truth?" He affected the worst Shakespearian accent she'd ever heard.

Switching lanes, she arched a brow. "You might have moves, but your accent sucks."

"Ouch. I might be wounded."

She glanced at him and took the Olive Way exit. "Sweetie, if I make the effort to intentionally wound you, you should just go ahead and prepare to bleed out."

"So noted."

Skyscrapers closed in around them as they made their way toward the Market. Streets narrowed and motorists were suddenly competing with cyclists, pedestrians, scooters and even the occasional Segway. With her window down to the surprisingly warm noonday sun, she listened as gulls circled and cried against the backdrop of an impossibly blue sky. Squadrons of pelicans moved parallel to the shoreline, their occasional rubber-against-glass bark of sound transcending humanity's noises. Mount Rainier loomed in the near distance, the recent snowfall leaving the north face brilliant above the cloud line. All in all, it was a perfect Seattle day. That meant Seattleites had come out en masse to enjoy the rare natural dose of vitamin D.

She pulled into a public parking garage and grabbed a ticket before winding her way up the levels until she found a decent spot on the third floor.

Dalton got out, met her at the rear of the car and took her hand, weaving their fingers together as he led her toward the bank of elevators where they caught a car to street level. When the car doors opened to the lobby, he pulled her through and into the sunshine like an anxious kid.

Even if she hadn't known that days like today were rare, the crush of people would have given something away. Residents of the 206 area code nearly had to take a blood oath asserting they'd get outside on sunny days if they wanted to have their utilities hooked up. The sidewalks were so crowded she couldn't comfortably walk beside Dalton. Instead, she let him clear the way, following in his wake. It made conversation impossible but afforded her time to think, and it was time she desperately needed.

They'd fallen into bed without realizing they were falling for each other, and she was sure it was happening for each of them. This wasn't some one-sided event. No, he'd made it clear he wanted this thing between them to grow, that he was willing to nurture it toward an exclusive—God save her—*relationship*. Hell, he'd somehow gone straight to "exclusive" without pause, convincing her they were on the same page. She still wasn't sure how it had happened. All she knew with certainty was that, according to Dalton and by her own admission, they were now in an exclusive relationship.

Butterflies cavorted behind her belly button, bouncing around all crazy and carefree as she continued along behind Dalton, her chin tucked in tight to her chest. Maybe the feeling wasn't carefree at all but rather totally panicked. That seemed more plausible, what with the slightly metallic taste on her tongue and the short, inefficient way her breath labored in and out of her chest. Yep, definitely panic.

Head down, she hadn't realized Dalton had stopped until she plowed into him, forcing him to take a step forward as he regained his balance.

He turned, grip on her hand still tight. "You okay?"

"Sorry. I wasn't watching." She tried to retrieve her hand, but he wasn't letting go.

"It's all good, but moves like that will get you a walk-on tryout for the Seahawks if they see you in action." He bent his head close to hers. "Between us, you've earned a fierce nickname," he said in a conspiratorial tone.

"I'm really sorry." She glanced around him, taking in the narrow stairway ahead as she tried to retrieve her hand. "Wait. What? What nickname?"

"Ariel."

Foot on the first step, she stopped and looked back, confused. "Ariel is hardly fierce."

"It's your affinity for barnacles."

The ridiculousness of the conversation almost made it make sense. Still… "Barnacles."

"You said it yourself—they're tenacious. As for the name, surely you've watched *The Little Mermaid*."

"Sure, but I have an excuse."

"Which is?"

"Ovaries. What's yours?"

"One of my best friends has two little sisters who're in training to become special-ops interrogators. They practiced on me one weekend, playing the soundtrack on repeat until I ended up in the fetal position under the dining room table answering every question they posed and some I might have imagined."

"I'm scared to ask," she said, laughing.

"Note to self—the woman finds torture hysterical," he muttered. Letting go of her hand, he wrapped an arm around her and encouraged her up the next step. "The appropriate response would be to offer to hold me until the flashbacks pass."

Deftly turning in his embrace, she found herself a step above him gazing down into laughter-filled green eyes. Her heart lurched with such force she actually staggered a bit.

His eyes flared. "What?"

"Nothing."

Taking her hand again, he traced a finger over the pad of her thumb. "So, you stumbling and gasping is a normal thing?"

"It's not even close to a 'thing.' It's not remotely a thing," she insisted, well aware she was lying to him because she didn't regularly stumble at the sight of a lovely pair of eyes. No, she definitely didn't. This was, in fact, a very terrifying first. "I just realized I have no idea why you're pushing me up a flight of stairs—"

"Two flights of stairs," he interjected.

"Fine. Two flights. You're pushing me up two flights of stairs. Why?"

"For the payoff."

She closed her eyes and took a steadying breath before slowly refocusing on Dalton's face. "I've been with you all morning and I fixed your coffee, so I'm pretty sure you haven't been drinking. Humor me and explain why we're here."

"We're here because my goal for the day is to ruin you for all other men."

Taking in the old stairwell and little shops tucked in the nooks and crannies, she couldn't help but smile. "We might need to talk about expectations. You know, yours versus mine."

She yelped when he smacked her on the ass.

Settling his hands on her hips, he turned her and urged her up the stairs again. "You'll rue the day you mocked me, woman."

"Mock? I don't mock."

Her feigned indignation was such a poor effort that a guy coming down the stairs actually snorted and patted her on the shoulder. "You'd have better luck selling milk back to the cow, gorgeous."

Her eyes nearly bugged out when Dalton burst out laughing as the stranger passed. "I'm using that one."

"If she's still fussy by the time she reaches the top of the stairs, she's not worth it, man."

Cass choked on her response.

Dalton's broad hand shifted to the base of her spine. "Oh, she's definitely worth it."

The guy tipped his head in acknowledgment, skipped down the last few steps and pushed through the lobby door to disappear into the foot traffic.

Managing, barely, to stifle her snarky response, she started up the stairs, mentally dressing the stranger down with extraordinary skill she'd never manage if she actually opened her mouth.

"Take a deep breath, Cass. He was only playing."

"Sure."

"I mean it." He hooked a finger through her belt loop and pulled her to a stop. "Look at me."

She glanced back, wary of his quiet surety.

"If he'd been disrespectful, I would have put a stop to it."

"With what? Witty repartee?" Words that should have come out teasing were soft and almost flat.

"I would have started there, yes. If it had taken more... persuasive measures, I'd have done that, too." He tucked a rogue wave of hair behind her ear. "No one disrespects you in front of me, baby."

One corner of her mouth kicked up in a tremulous smile. "Is that your version of 'nobody puts Baby in a corner'?"

He stepped up onto the next step so they were face-to-face before lowering his forehead to hers. "It's my way of proving what I said earlier—I'm on your side, Cass."

She shook her head gently and pulled away just far enough so she could meet his stare. "You paid that guy to say that to me, didn't you? Just now. He's an actor, and this is part of your plan to ruin me for all other men, using classic movie references to break down my defenses."

"I wish I could claim I'd done that because it would

have been brilliant." He took her hands and lifted her fingers to his lips for a quick, hard kiss. "Unfortunately, it was all improv."

Impulse drove her to lean in and take his mouth in a quick kiss. "You're a devious man, Dalton Chase."

"You have no idea."

Side by side, they started up the stairs. Halfway up the second flight, the soft, sweet scent of cooking pastry hit her. By the time they reached the second-floor landing, the area was infused with the smells of baking and chocolate and strong coffee. A vintage door with an oval glass pane and oval brass doorknob with a skeleton key port beneath it stood between her and what was undoubtedly, given the tantalizing smells, nirvana.

She looked over at Dalton. "There's no sign on the door."

"When you're as good as they are, you don't need a sign." With great relish, he pushed the door open and ushered Cass inside. "This, my lovely lady, is Le Crêpe Éprouver, home of the best crepes on the face of the planet."

"Crepes?"

His gaze roamed over the chalkboard list of daily specials as he answered. "You mentioned crepes the other day and I haven't been able to get them out of my mind since."

"Crepes."

"Yep. If I don't get me some strawberry and Nutella heaven, Seattle will fall into the sea as I unleash my wrath."

She widened her eyes with appropriate drama. "And here I thought I was safe with you."

"Never come between a man and his Nutella, baby."

"Duly noted." She stepped farther inside, and he closed

the door behind her. "If this place is half as amazing as it smells, you're one step closer to achieving my ruination."

"Wait until you taste their crepes. You'll be putty in my hands before I can feed you your second bite, woman."

Feed me. Her mind flashed some rather salacious images of Dalton, images that involved a ton of bare skin, some lemon curd and a can of whipped cream. She swallowed hard at the skin flick she was mentally directing and starring in. Sweat dotted her upper lip. Swiping at it surreptitiously was an act in casual indifference.

Dalton saw her.

His darkening gaze went from her mouth to her eyes. "What's on your mind, sweet Cass?"

"Lemon curd."

Reaching out, he cupped her chin and dragged a thumb along her cheekbone. "If you feel that strongly about lemon curd, I'll make sure you get it."

"I love it," she said, the declaration soft but unsure.

"Good to know." Pulling her to him, he settled his lips over hers in a breath-stealing kiss that completely disregarded their audience. The clink of forks on stoneware faded first, followed by the soft hum of diners' voices and the café employees' chatter until only the two of them existed.

Wrapping her arms around his neck, she poured everything she was into the kiss, tried to tell him without words that she was falling for him, hard and fast. Never in her life had she experienced anything like him. Never had she found anyone who made her feel so real and grounded and alive. Who she was in this moment meant more to him than who she'd ever been—a disappointment to her father, a woman lost to the demands of success, a failure in life outside the boardroom, a cursed Jameson by birth.

Things with Dalton were happening so fast, too fast,

completely out of control, and she didn't care. Cautious Cass no longer, she wanted more from him. She was desperate to find out what was on the other side of every second with him, hungry for that "more." There was so much potential inside these arms, so much room inside his heart and, surprisingly, hers. She'd never needed anyone. Not like this.

A lifetime of walls, walls she'd fought to keep in tact, crumbled. He'd done in days what no one else had been able to do in years. He had exposed her, left her completely vulnerable. It terrified her. Self-preservation demanded she shove him away and run until she couldn't breathe. Then run some more. Her heart demanded she stay invested in this very moment, hold him close and let him help her find the passion for life she'd squashed for so many years. He could. Only he could.

The knowledge made her knees buckle.

Dalton caught her. She'd been sure he would. In that moment, she was completely lost to him.

Unable to say the words, she gave all that she was to the kiss and uttered a silent prayer that Dalton would understand and respond in kind.

It wasn't the lemon curd she wanted. It was him. It wasn't the food she craved. It was him. It wasn't just his touch she needed. It was *him*.

All of him. She'd abandoned her obligations, her ambitions and her defenses. Now she had to believe his promise to keep her safe.

THE WOMAN ERIC held in his arms had become a living flame. That made him a moth, drawn inexplicably despite the surety that she'd be the death of him. Or maybe he found himself pulled in because he realized she had the potential to be the death of who he'd always been. Either way, he was lost to the inexorable draw of her. She'd been holding a piece of herself back, even in the most passionate moments between them, keeping herself in check. But now, in this moment, he had her. All of her. Damn if that didn't make him a hypocrite.

Fingers digging into her waist, he broke the kiss and leaned back only enough to search her eyes. They shone bright and clear, unguarded. What he found in them made him want to run. She deserved more than he'd ever been—a hustler, a brawler, now a stripper whose one chance to be more hung in a precarious balance. If he didn't make it happen, he'd never be more than the sum of his past.

But the way she was looking at him… He wanted to be the man he saw reflected in her eyes. More than anything, he wanted that. She empowered him, quietly encouraging him to simply be who he was without compromise and then to be more. It had been that way from the moment she'd told him to go to the woman at the bachelorette party whose husband had left her, to flirt a little and encourage the woman to feel beautiful. Cass had done that without judgment, without jealousy. If he was going to be honest, that had been the beginning of the end for him. That had been the very second he'd begun to fall for her. Now? He was caught in a blind free fall, the kind that shoved your stomach into the back of your throat and made your brain press against the top of your skull. He loved it, even if he was damned for it.

Adrenaline surfing his blood stream, Eric realized with a gut-wrenching certainty he was done running. He'd spent a lifetime chasing shadows and dreams, moving from one person or project to the next, always searching for that next "thing," that next hit that would get him through the night. Happiness had been elusive and, at times, so far out of reach he'd simply stopped reaching. But now, with Cass gazing at him with such fierce and unguarded hope, he wanted to be the man she seemed to think he was.

He pulled her impossibly closer, resting his cheek against her temple as he breathed her in. His heart beat hard and sure.

No more chasing dreams he couldn't see. The one he had in his arms was better than anything he'd come up with on his own. He would find his happiness here. He'd have to find the right moment to say he'd fallen for her. The absolute last thing he wanted was for her to run, to tell him it was too much too soon. It wasn't. What he felt for her was irrefutable. His job was to convince her he was the best man to care for her. She could argue any angle she wanted, but the truth was the truth.

His fingers dug into her hips hard enough that her eyes flared. "Dalton?"

Truth. A single lie existed between them, and he would change that. He wouldn't have her committing to Dalton Chase when it was Eric Reeves who cared about her. He should have told her that first night. He knew he should have. But the risks had been too high that she could ruin his career, and then afterward, it had been too high that she would break his heart if, or when, she left. Now the risk was that he'd hurt her by revealing his ridiculous lies. And he still had no idea how to avoid that, the worst consequence of all.

His conscience continued to beat the ever-loving shit out of him as he stood there staring at Cass. As he opened his mouth to start to explain, the creperie's door pushed open and knocked him into her. They stumbled to the side, crashing into the menu board. He scrambled to keep her upright as he reached for the teetering chalkboard.

A second pair of hands reached over and grabbed the board. "Oh, man, I'm sorry. I didn't see—hey, man! Haven't seen you here in forever. You enter a twelve-step Nutella program or something?"

Eric spun around to find Levi grinning at him. His heart stopped. Just bloody stopped. Levi was one of only two people he hadn't wanted to run into here. He'd assumed he'd be safe this morning because Levi was never up this early. Until today. *Damn it.*

Cass pulled her hands away and stepped around him. "I'm going to go out on a limb and guess that you guys know each other." Her gaze moved over Levi appreciatively but without heat.

"We work together," Eric blurted, jealousy digging its wicked claws into his back between his shoulder blades. "Cass, this is Levi, lead exotic dancer and general go-to man at the club." It struck Eric as brutally wrong that he'd introduced Levi under his real name while he, Eric, couldn't give Cass the same courtesy. He was so going to screw this up.

Taking a deep breath, he dropped an arm casually around Cass's shoulders to interrupt Levi's undisguised perusal of, and appreciation for, her body. She stiffened slightly, and he pulled her close. "Put your eyes back in your head and roll your tongue up, my man. This one's…" He'd started to say "off the market," but it was too presumptuous. He had to hear the words from Cass before he would throw that out there and maybe get shot down.

His jaw tightened at that last thought. There was no way she would shoot him down. The look in her eyes before Levi—

"You okay?"

Her voice dragged him out of the swirling mass of

thick emotion that threatened to squeeze the air out of his lungs. A brief nod was the best he could do.

Levi stepped in and held out a hand. "It's nice to meet you, Cass."

She took the proffered hand with confidence. "You, too."

"I really am sorry about mowing you guys down." Levi's grin was one part wicked and one part angelic. "I hit the gym early. As a result, I'm not only starving but moving on an endorphin high that sort of had me plowing into the room."

An uncharacteristic flush of color stole across his cheeks as Cass focused on him, and Eric managed a choked laugh.

"Anyway, I'm sorry." Levi jerked his head toward the counter. "You guys order already?"

"No, but Dalton has promised me lemon curd crepes that will make me his slave for life. I refuse to leave until I get them."

Levi looked at him and arched a brow. "*Dalton* did, huh?"

Eric gave a short nod, fighting to regain control of the moment. "Don't hate on me because of the woman on my arm." He grinned. "She's totally my type, and that makes her not yours."

That was as clear as Eric could get in telling Levi to keep his meaty paws to himself. The man had a reputation as a sexual shark, and Eric didn't want there to be any misunderstanding regarding Cass. He also didn't want Levi to give him away. The guy didn't believe in anything but the most casual of relationships, and he might consider screwing up Eric's thing with Cass to be in his friend's best interest.

After what felt like forever, Levi gave a short nod.

Cass glanced between them, her brow wrinkled. "Why do I feel like you guys are having a telepathic conversation I should be part of?"

Eric ran his hand around her neck and turned her toward him. He moved in, settling his free hand on her hip and moving his mouth over hers in a short, soft but proprietary kiss. "It's nothing."

Levi cleared his throat. "I'm going to grab my order to go. Cass, please accept my apologies for nearly knocking you on your—" he grinned at Eric "—very fine ass. I hope to see more of you."

Cass laughed. "It was nice to meet you, too, Levi."

Nodding at Eric, the other man wove through the tables to reach the counter. His deep voice joined the murmur of other diners as they went back to their meals.

Eric looked down at the woman still held so securely in his arms. "You okay?"

"I'm fine. You? You seem a little rattled."

"Just didn't want to see you knocked around, particularly by one of my friends." He shook his head. "Levi's usually much smoother than that."

She huffed out a breath. "He'd have to be if he was going to give a woman a lap dance without killing her."

Eric's bark of laughter made Levi glance over his shoulder, a slow grin spreading across his face. He slid a finger across his throat, miming a slicing motion.

Lifting a shoulder, Eric realized the guy was right.

He was doomed.

THEY GRABBED A late brunch before heading out again. Eric had waffled on what to do next. Spending any more money over the weekend would be painful because he still had to sort out the mess with his brother's tuition. Sovereign's board of directors was coming in later this week, which meant a nice meal out somewhere on the company's—his—dime. And he couldn't ignore his car since it seemed to be on its deathbed. Then again, anything that endeared Cass to him before he told her the truth would be worth it.

Muttering a vicious curse, he pulled his cell phone from his back pocket. He went with his gut and did what felt right, ordering tickets to see *Grease* at the 5th Avenue Theater while Cass was in the ladies' room.

A few hours later, Eric was convinced he'd made the right call. He'd remembered she had a soft spot for musicals, and while the show had been awesome, her response had been even better. He'd had as much fun watching her reactions as he'd had watching the performers and singing along with the songs.

Afterward, they'd wandered through Pike's Place Market and he'd bought her a huge bouquet of spring flowers. He'd considered the roses first, but they weren't "her." The spring flowers, though... They'd been cultivated but had a wild quality about them, and they spoke to him. He'd laughed at himself when he picked them up. When he handed them to Cass, her reaction nailed his heart to his chest. She'd been quiet, burying her face in the soft petals and just breathing. He'd reached for her at the same time she'd looked up, eyes swimming in tears. He'd crushed the flowers between them as he tunneled his fingers through her hair and hauled her up to her tiptoes, lowering his mouth to hers. He lost himself in her, immune to the worries of everyday life and the crush of people murmuring around them, aware the magic of the weekend was winding down as real life loomed on the other side of midnight.

For the first time in his life, Eric felt a little sorry for Cinderella.

He thought of the coming week's fight with the board to fund his development project despite an engineering plan that was severely over budget. Then he considered Cass's reaction when he revealed that he'd been keeping his name and even part of his identity hidden from her. He was facing ruination on both sides. Not to mention she'd said she had her own big meeting later this week that he didn't want to affect.

What could delaying the truth a few more days hurt?

14

ERIC ROLLED OVER in time to see a naked ass—a very *fine* naked ass—disappear into his bathroom for the fourth day in a row. She'd stayed at his place since their outing Sunday. They'd each gone to work, with her leaving before he did every day. He was home earlier, too, anxious to be there when she walked through the door. He was totally gone on her and loving every minute. Speaking of minute, he glanced at the clock and winced. A few minutes after five. In the morning. No one should have to get up this damn early. Groaning, he flopped onto his back and flung an arm over his eyes to block the bathroom light. The disturbed air brought with it the faint hint of perfume from her side of the bed.

Her side of the bed.

Man, he liked how that sounded. He rolled over again, burying his face in her pillow and breathing deep of the signature scent that was all her—perfume combined with shampoo, expensive hairspray and something that was faintly all her own.

They'd gone to bed early every night but fallen asleep so late he had no idea how she was still functioning. Talking between bouts of nearly crazed lovemaking, they'd learned so much about each other. Little things, such as the fact she loved Jif whipped chocolate peanut butter-and-banana sandwiches. That he had grown up wanting to be a pilot but had never flown anything more than a kite. That she wanted a dog in the worst way but felt she didn't have the space or time for the breed she wanted. That his favorite food was Alaskan king crab. That she hated seafood with a passion. All kinds of similarities and differences that made her so real to him, seating her in his heart in a way that should have taken months and months of effort yet had been nearly immediate and absolutely effortless.

By some unspoken agreement, neither of them talked about their day job.

As Dan had warned, on Monday the engineers had confirmed EPA approval of their plan, but had informed Sovereign that the plan would cost significantly more than originally forecast. He'd never met the engineering team—the bids had been blind to prevent unethical behavior. But they'd be there for the meeting with the board, pushing their plan. Which was just as well, since he needed all the help he could get to convince the board to pony up even more money. But all of that was stress he didn't want to bring into his relationship with Cass, and besides, judging how tired she was when she came home, she didn't need it.

The pipes rattled a little beneath the floor when Cass turned on the shower, and he heard the sound of the curtain being pulled closed seconds before he heard her curses.

Shifting to his side, he listened and grinned. "You always forget that it takes a few minutes for the water heater to get chugging," he shouted.

"I hate you," she called out.

He had no idea if she was talking to him or the water heater. It didn't matter. He was so damn happy he wouldn't have cared if it had all been directed at him.

Sleep reclaimed him somewhere between that last thought and the fundamental understanding he'd completely fallen for this woman in a matter of days. He woke sometime later to fingers threading through his hair and soft lips at his temple.

"I have to go home and get some clothes. I'm already out of what I brought over Sunday."

Sighing, he fought the urge to slip back into the dream he'd been caught up in. The bed shifted as she moved away. "You should call in, spend the day with me," he murmured, face still half pressed into the pillow. *Her* pillow.

A smile hovered in her answer. "And what would we do?"

"Each other."

This time she laughed. "I have a monster-ass meeting today."

"Monster ass, huh? I'm no competition when I'm up against *that* kind of entertainment." He rolled onto his side, rubbing his face with one hand. "It was wishful thinking, anyway. My day is packed with stuff I can't get out of." Even if he wanted to. And he did.

Soft lips traveled down his cheek and rested near his chin. "I'd love to stay here. I doubt this meeting is going to go well. Apparently the CEO we'll be presenting to today is a real dick."

"Call me when you're out. We'll grab lunch. Or each other. Whatever."

She laughed, hot breath skating across his skin.

"Oh, and Cass?"

"Yes?"

"If the guy's that much of a dick, be sure to practice safe business."

This time her laughter rolled out in peals, the sound warming him even as he slid back into sleep. He was going to miss her this morning, but he had his own mountains to climb.

His stomach rolled over as his heart thundered inside his chest like Thor's hammer. Panic stole his breath and turned his liver to mush. It struck every nerve, hammering at him until his hands fisted and his muscles cramped in a full-body charley horse.

His primary concern was the board approving the engineer's proposal, a proposal he couldn't afford to fund without more money from his investors. He'd have to get them to dig into their own coffers to come up with the difference between what he had in available cash and assets versus what the proposal mandated. And they weren't going to like it.

He didn't want to deal with the board today. The potential for financial devastation and the loss of his dream had no business crowding out the happiness, the sense of settled belonging he'd finally found. One false step and he'd be screwed. He'd just have to ensure that didn't happen. No matter what.

LOST IN THOUGHT, Cass walked through the parking garage attached to her apartment building. She'd experienced so much over the past six days with Dalton she was feeling out of sorts—calm yet giddy, scared yet thrilled, lost yet found. So completely found. Never in her life had she been so sure of her place, and that place was with Dalton. Every moment with him was saturated with life, complete in a way that let her know she hadn't been entirely complete before. She hadn't been unhappy. That wasn't it. It was that, when she was with Dalton, she was *more*. She was *better*. He took the shades of black and white her life had always been and added bold strokes of color and dimension, created depth and movement. He made her feel alive in a way she'd never experienced before. He made her feel loved.

She was exactly who she wanted to be when she was with him. It truly didn't matter he was a stripper. It didn't matter he didn't have money or a hefty portfolio or connections to families that would strengthen the Jameson empire. Those were all things her father wanted, even expected. They weren't who she was. Dalton had none of the things her father demanded of her suitors, and that thrilled her. This man, *her* man, was everything she needed, everything she wanted, and all on her own terms. He hadn't come to her seeking to gain something through a strategic relationship or, heaven save her, marriage. He hadn't come to her planning to use her to get closer to her father and his influence. No. Dalton had come to her of his own accord. He'd bared himself to her and shown her what it was to be loved.

Overcome, she threw her arms wide and spun in a circle, head back and eyes closed as she laughed. She'd completely fallen for him, heart and soul.

Her hands slammed into somebody and she yanked them back, stumbling to regain her balance. "I'm so sorry! I didn't mean to—"

Strong hands gripped her shoulders. "Forgiven." Lips crushed hers in a bruising kiss.

She returned the kiss for a split second, thinking that Dalton had followed her home for some reason. Then it registered—the taste of expensive cigars and smooth whiskey, the texture of lips that were too thin, the smell of Clive Christian No. 1, the feel of wool and cashmere beneath her fingers—this wasn't Dalton.

Fighting to free herself, she wrenched her mouth to the side and gasped. Then the self-defense classes Gwen had insisted they take for their first couple of years in Seattle kicked in. She screamed as loud as she could in her assailant's ear. When he jerked back, she head butted him, a satisfying grunt the man's only response. His hands tightened on her arms, so she stomped on his insole and attempted to knee him in the groin as hard as she could. He twisted at the last second, though, and she struck thigh as much as testicles. Still, the man crumpled like an empty gunnysack.

Cass stumbled away, fighting to keep from blindly running and putting herself in more danger by pinning herself in.

"Damn it, Cass!" Blue eyes blazed beneath dark brows and a trendy executive haircut that was now thoroughly out of sorts. "What the hell is your problem?"

"Marcus?" she asked blinking rapidly. "Why… What was that about?" The longer she stood there catching her breath, the angrier she became. "What in God's name gave you the impression I'd be fine with you assaulting me? No, don't answer that. I don't want to know what twisted little game you've cooked up this time. The answer is, and will always be, no. Not only no, but *hell* no. So pack up your poster-pretty image and scuttle home to my father. Tell him I'll be passing on his latest attempt at matchmaking. I've managed just fine on my own." Fury made her stupid, and the words were out before she realized she'd given the pair something to use against her. Cursing herself, she spun on her heel and started for the elevators.

A viselike grip locked on her upper arm and hauled

her around. Momentum slammed her into Marcus's body. "Heads up? I haven't been screwing that lifeless assistant of yours for nothing." He laughed when her eyes widened. "It's amazing what a woman will say and do when she thinks a man gives a damn about her. I know enough about Preservations to take over when the time comes."

"Don't hold your breath," Cass snapped, pulling against his hold. "You'll never have that position."

"No, *you* listen, you little bitch. I've earned this position with your father, and he agreed you were part of my compensation package. So I'm not about to let you go and screw it all up. You *won't* throw me over for some twenty-buck, lap-dancing, lying male whore who offers you cheap flowers and a three-dollar bottle of wine with your Olive Garden takeout."

Her stomach launched itself into her throat as if it had been emergency ejected. Swallowing bile, she shook her head. "You don't know what you're talking about." But he did. Her assistant, a woman she had trusted with so much, had sold her out. And for what? What had he promised her? Just another example of men lying and cheating to get what and where they wanted.

Then there was Dalton. Everything Marcus had mentioned in his oily diatribe had been something she'd experienced with Dalton. True, wildflowers weren't expensive, but she'd loved them because he'd chosen something different for her. They'd ordered takeout from Olive Garden so they could sit in bed and watch the newest Jeff Dunham comedy special. And the wine *had* been cheap, but it had been spontaneous and fun and she'd licked the flavor from Dalton's lips and—

Marcus shook her hard enough her head snapped back. "Your little Magic Mike isn't who you think he is."

"You leave Dalton out of this," she snarled.

Marcus's eyebrows winged up. "Dalton? Did he say that was his name?" He roared with laughter, shaking so hard he actually let her go to grip his side. Cass shoved him back with a hard shot to the shoulder, but he kept laughing.

Whirling away from him, she stalked across the parking lot. *Stairs or elevator?* Either way, she didn't want to end up trapped somewhere with Marcus. She was pissed to admit he'd scared and confused her. Badly. Her heels clipped across the concrete, pounding out a harsh rhythm a hairbreadth from a run.

"He's lying to you, Cass."

She flipped Marcus the bird, never slowing down.

"Just remember that I warned you when this all blows up in your face," he said just loudly enough for her to hear him. "And it will."

"Stay away from me, Marcus." Punching the down button for the elevator, she glanced over her shoulder, surprised to see him standing where he'd been, hands in his pockets, and grinning. "Next time you come anywhere near me, I'll get a restraining order. How long do you think dear ol' Dad will keep you on when you become a public relations liability?" She tapped her lips with one finger as she feigned deep thought. She dropped her hand from her mouth and stared at him with abject hatred. "I've watched more of your kind come and go in the past few years than you can imagine. You're no different from the last three Jameson let go, so don't go fooling yourself you're different or special. You're replaceable, because there are a hundred more like you dogging your heels."

The elevator doors opened and she stepped inside, frantically pressing the close button as Marcus started after her. If she ended up trapped in here with him, if he pushed the emergency stop, if he wasn't lying and her father had done just what he'd said and offered her up as some kind of prize—

The doors slid shut with a soft hiss, and the car began its descent. At the third floor, she started shaking. Black spots danced across her vision and she wondered, briefly, if she was going to faint for the first time in her life.

"No," she ground out, bending at the waist and forcing herself to breathe slow and deep.

The elevator stopped at her floor and the doors opened. Cass stood, steadied herself and then walked out as if nothing had happened, heading straight for her apartment.

Letting herself in, she closed the door and leaned against it. She was home. It felt good, if a little empty without Dalton. A soft beep made her glance at her phone. The voice mail was blinking rapidly.

She grabbed the handset and dialed.

"Front desk, Madeline speaking."

"Hey, Madeline. It's Cass Wheeler. You left me a message to call the front desk for a pickup?"

"Yes, ma'am. You have a delivery."

Dread curled through her, its fingers impossibly cold. "I haven't ordered anything."

"Oh, it's not that kind of delivery." The woman, younger than the concierge Cass had argued with before, couldn't contain her unabashed enthusiasm. "It's the kind of delivery every woman wants to come home to."

The memory of wildflowers crushed between her and Dalton made her heart skip a beat. "Flowers?"

"I'll say. There are at least three-dozen long-stemmed roses here in a cut crystal vase. They're over-the-top, Ms. Jameson. Whoever sent them surely intended to impress you. I'd say he succeeded."

Cass swallowed hard through her constricting throat. She didn't have to read the card to be sure they weren't from Dalton. He wouldn't have sent her something that didn't suit her. He knew her too well.

But how well did she know him? Marcus had been too damn smug not to know something she didn't. He'd been way too confident this was going to blow up in her face.

"Ms. Jameson? Should I have them delivered or would you like to come pick them up?"

"Keep them," Cass whispered.

Numb, she resumed the trek through her apartment, all the while trying to ignore the devastating feeling Marcus had been telling her the truth.

About all of it.

15

CASS STOOD IN the Caston Building's parking garage fighting to breathe. She hadn't had a full-blown panic attack in more than two years, but this little band-around-the-chest-I'm-having-a-heart-attack feeling promised to be a doozy. *Stupid, fracking Marcus. It's all his fault.* And it was. If he hadn't worked her up about Dalton, she'd be fine—or at least able to breathe.

Chewing her bottom lip, she absently picked at a cuticle, a nervous habit. She forced herself to stop. She couldn't go into the presentation with ragged fingers. That would be just fantastic— she put so much effort into looking like the Ice Princess she'd been dubbed only to have her rough fingers relay her nerves loud and clear. Right. Fantastic.

Taking several deep breaths, she shook out her hands and did a quick assessment. Skirt was zipped. She ran her hands around her waist and hips. No strange bulges where her shirt was tucked in. Except… Crap. There was always one part of her shirt that wadded up and needed to be smoothed at the last minute. Opening her car door, she half crouched behind it and ran her hand up her skirt, fishing for the shirttail. Fear that someone would see her was a far second to her fear that somehow Marcus was watching. As always, her father had found a way to influence her life.

Stealth proved useless. She stood and twisted herself into an approximation of an origami swan as she bent and pushed and pulled to get everything just right, then had to fix her bra as a result. Pinpricks of sweat dotted her brow when all was said and done.

"Damn it." The low epithet was issued softly and for her benefit only. *Words. Simply words.* But they allowed her to vent a little of the building pressure.

"Stressing out?"

Cass spun around so hard and fast she bounced her hip off the neighboring car. "Damn it!" This time the epithet was yelled. "Don't do that to me."

Gwen shrugged. "Look. I'm getting married in seventy-two hours. I've got so much more stress on me right now than you do, there's no way you're getting any sympathy. *Capisce?*"

Heart in her throat, Cass nodded. "You're right. I know you're right. It's only…"

Gwen moved close and hugged Cass. "This deal isn't about you besting your father. It isn't about you one-upping him in the real estate world or showing him you've arrived or anything else you might be thinking."

"I can't help but feel like I'm aiding and abetting the enemy. I found out how my father always seems to know my movements. I'm scared he's going to somehow use me to win the project back from Sovereign."

"What? What happened?" Gwen demanded.

So Cass explained, all about Marcus, from him following her to his crazed pursuit of her.

Gwen ran a hand up and down Cass's arm and stared

up at her, eyes solemn. "You should've called me. I would've come over so you didn't have to face this alone."

That was part of the issue. She could've called Gwen, but she hadn't. She'd wanted to call Dalton, had even gone so far as to pick up the phone. But she hadn't called him, either. Scared he'd come down on her for making something out of nothing, that he'd sound like her father and ruin what she felt for him, had terrified her. And, if she was totally honest, Marcus had succeeded in planting a kernel of doubt in her heart where Dalton was concerned.

Gwent laid a hand on her arm. "Cass?"

"I'm fine." She shook her head. "It's fine."

"No, it's not. Listen to me," Gwent said, an undercurrent of rage fueling her words. "You could've handed the project to your father if you'd wanted to. You could've made it impossible for Sovereign to possibly gain the EPA's approval, and then turned the project over to your father. You didn't. You let the process go through each phase, respected the rules of the system and let the bidding fall as it would. The developers could have chosen another environmental firm to handle the runoff issues. They liked our proposal best.

"And as for your assistant? We'll deal with her when this meeting is done."

"But—"

"No," Gwen snapped. "Stop it, Cass. You're going to second-guess every move we've made and go in there with doubts. Stop it." Gwen paused, considering Cass intently. "You've always been the stronger of the two of us. Where's this coming from? What's going on?"

Cass rolled her lips in to stop herself from picking at her fingernails again.

Gwen crossed her arms and stared at her with a fierce glare that spelled trouble. "Spill, woman."

"I've been with Dalton."

"I know." The petite blonde waggled her eyebrows. "You've been tight-lipped about things with him since you met him."

Cass closed her eyes and forced herself to breathe around her heart that had firmly lodged itself in her throat. "It's more than just being with him, Gwen."

"Hey. What's going on?"

No way was Cass ready for this conversation. She just couldn't. It was all too raw, too *real* to deal with right now. "We can talk about it after the presentation."

"We're almost forty-five minutes early. We can take fifteen minutes to talk," Gwen said gently. "C'mon." Grabbing her wrist, Gwen pulled her to the back of the Preservations' truck that Cass had driven this morning. Dropping the tailgate and hopping up, she crossed her legs with a deliberate scissor kick and gestured grandly for Cass to join her.

Cass couldn't help but smile. "This is your version of a therapist's couch?"

"A woman must use the tools available to her. That means this is my confidential office and, by default, this is, indeed, my couch. Now, pull up a butt-crushing metal cushion and tell me what's going on."

Slipping onto the tailgate, Cass crossed her legs and leaned back on her hands. Instinct had her surveying the area for Marcus. She couldn't believe he'd simply leave her be. Not after this morning. Gwen needed to know what was happening no matter how much it humiliated Cass.

She reached up to run her hands through her hair and remembered she'd put it up in a tight chignon. Fidgeting with her skirt hem instead, she sighed. "Let me sum it up for you. I've had the best six days of my life, and they started when Dalton walked through my apartment door. Yes, there's been sex—*amazing* sex—but that's not it. Or, at least, it's not all of it." She stopped fidgeting and brought her fingertips to her lips, smiling. "We laugh and talk way too late into the night, though we're still dancing around some of the finer points of our lives. No skeletons out of the closet, I guess. Just talk. There's no pressure on me about being a Jameson. He doesn't want me for any reason other than because I'm me. *Me,* Gwen. *Just* me. My family isn't part of some sexual negotiation. It's just us in that bedroom.

"And then? The other day? We went to the Market and he bought me wildflowers before we got takeout and Two-Buck Chuck and went back to his place to eat, drink and watch *Phantom of the Opera* in bed."

"*Phantom,* huh? He's pulling out the big guns."

"He knows I love musicals, and he likes them, too." She shifted onto her hip and, propping herself on one hand, said what she'd been so afraid to say. "He fills this part of me I didn't even realize was empty, Gwen. It's as if he's the only thing in life I was missing, and it scares the hell out of me. I don't know that I need him, exactly, but I want him. Desperately."

Gwen slid off the tailgate and stood, offering Cass her hand. When she hesitated, Gwen wiggled her fingers. "Come here."

Cass went to her feet and took Gwen's hand.

"When I met Dave, there was this…this…*connection.* He plugged into a hollow part of me and I was suddenly energized. Things were better because he was with me, no matter what they were. Oh, I would have been fine without him. I could have lived and been happy. But now I'm happier. Life's just better with him than it is without."

"Exactly." Cass nodded vigorously.

Gwen stroked a thumb over Cass's hand. "You're still you—independent, strong, goal-oriented. You're just finding more strength in being with him than in being without. And you're a fool if you walk away from that out of fear."

The fear comment made the skin on the back of Cass's neck crawl. "I think a little fear is justified. Marcus dropped a vague warning about Dalton. I didn't get it, and I didn't stick around to ask questions."

Gwen's eyes narrowed as she smiled. "I want to stick that asshole in a tiny cage with a very angry, male-hating, extremely hungry lioness with only half her teeth so she can gnaw on him awhile."

Cass nervously nodded. "You scare me a little."

"I'd rather scare him." The petite blonde sighed. "Marcus Assholius aside, you mentioned fear. You don't have to be so afraid of falling in love, sweetie."

"I'm not f-falling…" She stuttered to a stop. Love? No. This wasn't love with Dalton. Not yet. It was very intense like and electric chemistry, yes. But love? Love took time.

Gwen glanced at her watch. "We need to do a quick review before we go in there, give you a chance to get your mind back in the game. We'll deal with your assistant and Marcus later. And, for what it's worth…I know how it feels to be right there on the cusp of falling. It's scary as hell. But the actual fall?" She grinned, her eyes bright. "There's nothing like it."

Fear wrestled with hope, a slippery, Jell-O tub fight to the bitter end in her mind. It was a visual mess. She let her eyes slip closed and thought of Dalton, of leaving his sleepy form in bed this morning. He'd smiled at her, tempting her to stay in so many ways. Everything about him made her want to be with him more, to have him in her life on a more permanent basis.

"But what if I'm not sure I want to fall? What if I'm not entirely sure whom I'm falling for? Like I said, no skeletons out of the closet yet."

"Falling is only part choice, sweetie. But that choice requires bravery and faith," Gwen said so softly Cass had to focus to hear her. "You've always been brave. As for the faith? If he's captured the most elusive part of you? Find faith in him. Don't lose him to cowardice and distrust."

Toes curled over the edge of that terrifying precipice, Cass opened herself to the possibilities and leaped.

She was officially falling in love with Dalton Chase.

16

ERIC PACED THE length of his office. Less than an hour until the moment of truth that would either carry him away in a rush of success or roll over him and leave him as broken and disregarded as roadkill. He huffed. The roadkill analogy might be a little strong, he supposed. A negative outcome wouldn't kill him, but it would undoubtedly drive him to wish it had. He couldn't imagine telling his assistant, whose husband had just lost his job, that she too was losing hers. Or facing down his project manager and explaining to her that she'd have to sort out the unemployment process as well as the unexpected divorce filing by her husband. Particularly hard would be informing his development analyst, a friend he'd recruited straight out of college, that his first job reference would come from a defunct company. Not much to analyze in that.

On the next pass by his desk, Eric grabbed his roll of antacids and popped a couple. The chalky grit didn't bother him anymore. Hell, these things were the equivalent of after-dinner mints to him now.

He stopped—stopped pacing, stopped chewing, stopped stewing—as his mind went to the conversation with Cass where she'd allowed herself to be vulnerable and he'd made some inane comment about after-dinner mints. Warmth bloomed inside him. She'd smiled at him then, laughed even, and it had spurred him down the reckless road that led him here, to this moment.

It dawned on him that the success of this meeting meant a great deal to the success of their relationship. If he could stop saving soda bottle caps for the freebies, stop fearing every check he wrote would bounce, stop freaking stripping, he could stop focusing on the immediate crises in his life and actually start looking ahead. Without that choice, there was no future for them. He couldn't pay for the rare nice dinner in ones and occasional fives and not be reminded of how he'd almost made it. He couldn't explain that in a few years, when younger guys took over as the premier dancers, he'd be job hunting with an outdated degree and no viable résumé. She'd understand the concept, but the reality would leave her bitter and resentful. That was something he wouldn't risk. He'd cut her free first.

"What the hell?" he grumbled, giving his executive's chair a hard shot to the backrest that sent it careening across his office and bouncing off the far wall. Snatching up his coffee cup, he lifted it but didn't drink as he stared out across the plans for the modest business development. He hadn't lost the deal, yet here he stood, sucking down shit for his stomach problems, mentally laying off staff and cutting Cass loose? "Get your shit together, Reeves. You didn't get this far by being the chick who trips in the woods in every slasher flick. You've done the legwork. You've worked all the angles. You managed to outmaneuver David Jameson. You've proved your better than this. You're smarter than this." He snorted into his cup and muttered, "And by golly, people like you."

Stripped Down

He took a sip of lukewarm coffee and wondered for the hundredth time what Cass was doing this morning, how her meeting was going. Hopefully her prep work had paid off. He'd never seen a woman as driven to succeed. They hadn't talked about their daily lives much. Not yet, anyway. There had been too much to learn about each other in every moment, too much to process about who they were without the bullshit of job titles and salaries and career tracks. And, if he were honest, he hadn't wanted her to know about the very real possibility he might lose his shirt because he simply wasn't good enough to hang on to it.

The truth, finally faced, delivered his ego a particularly brutal blow. He lost his shirt for money four nights a week, and now here he stood, fighting to keep it at all costs.

Tipping his head back, he laughed at the same time someone knocked on his door. "Come in," he called, grinning as he set the dregs of his coffee on his desk.

His assistant stepped inside with her steno pad and the ever-present pen stuck behind her ear. "You wanted to be informed when the board arrived. Mr. Declan just got off the elevator. He's in the restroom." She adjusted her glasses. "The boardroom is set up and ready to go, and the engineers should be here soon. Do you still want the board assembled before the engineers are shown in?"

This was the first gamble of the day. Bringing the engineers into the room with the board present and seated meant the presenters would have to be on their game the second they hit the doorway. Letting the engineers get settled and then bringing the board in put his team at a bit of a disadvantage on the power grid, and there was no mistaking the fact this would be a meeting where power and influence shaped the outcome.

Shoving his hands in his pockets, he rocked back and forth, heel to toe. "Yeah, let's put our people in first. I'll go now, pick up Declan on the way. Leave the engineers in the reception area even if you have to call the board members in one at a time. I don't want the people from Preservations to enter the room until our team is fully assembled." He adjusted his tie before retrieving his chair and pulling his suit jacket off the back and shrugging into it. "Let them stew a little. Before you escort them into the boardroom, I want you to come in and quietly tell me they've arrived. It's all set up, but it's about making sure we're ready. You okay with that?"

She smiled and nodded. "It's not my first strategic hoedown."

"I didn't realize hoedowns could be strategic," he teased, starting for the door.

She shrugged. "Depends on who's leading the band, I suppose."

He chuckled and strode out of his office to find Mr. Declan waiting for him. Extending a hand, Eric began what would hopefully be the first of many stressful days as Chok Resort came into being under the guidance and development of his team and these people's money.

REVELATIONS ABOUT FALLING in love weren't enough to intercept Cass's temper as the morning wore on. She was pissed. The CEO was proving himself to be just as much of an asshole as she'd heard he was, leaving her and Gwen sitting in the reception area for the past twenty minutes as, one by one, a pretty, middle-aged woman took an all-male cast of fifty-five-plus men back to the boardroom. The guy was probably trying to psyche her out, giving her a glimpse of the moneyed players without letting her in on their game plan. If the jackass had ever sat through one of her family's dinner parties, he'd realize how futile his efforts were. No one intimidated like her father, no one shamed as well as her mother, and no one rained disdain as efficiently as her brother. She'd had way too much experience in this particular arena to let the guy get to her. And the anxious bride at her side? Cass wasn't about to bet on anyone but Gwen when they entered the apparently to-be-revered environment of the holy boardroom. Her best friend would be a professional terror.

Gwen leaned over and nudged Cass, tilting her head toward the door to the inner sanctum of the offices. "Think he has a small penis?"

"Huh?"

"The CEO. He's sure putting on a show, leaving us out here to sweat it out."

She laughed. "I was just thinking the same thing." Wiping damp palms on her skirt, it irritated her that he was getting under her skin a little. "We're ready, though."

They fist-bumped at the same time the now familiar woman returned for them.

"If you'll come with me, I'll deliver you to the board of directors for your presentation."

As a unit, Cass and Gwen stood, briefcases in hand and spines straight.

"Thank you," Cass said, tipping her head in acknowledgment.

They followed the assistant down a short hallway, stopping in front of a heavy door.

"One moment, please," the woman said, slipping into the room.

Gwen sniffed the air and turned to Cass. "Smell that?"

Cass's brow wrinkled and she sniffed. "What?"

"The testosterone. It's choking me to death. I must be

more susceptible because I'm shorter and that crap is so heavy it hovers low to the ground."

Laughter choked Cass, forcing her to press her lips together and fight to keep her composure when their tour guide came out again.

"They're ready for you."

Cass took a steadying breath and stepped inside, Gwen right on her heels.

The room was generic in appearance—pale gray walls, dark gray carpet, heavy wooden table with high-backed leather chairs filled with predictably benign faces. All but one. The chair at the head of the table was facing the other way, toward the plans mounted on the wall. The CEO, Eric Reeves.

Papers shuffled.

Someone cleared his throat.

The CEO spun his chair at the same time Cass started to say, "Gentlemen," but she managed only, "Gentleme—" before coming to a faltering stop.

Blood pounded in her ears like a tribal drumbeat. Black dots danced across her vision and she blinked rapidly. A cold bead of sweat raced down the hollow of her spine even as her mouth went drier than the Sahara at the height of summer. It wasn't possible. This wasn't happening to her.

Betrayed.

She'd taken the freaking leap of faith only an hour ago. The universe wouldn't be so cruel as to let her land flat on her face. Oh, but it felt as if everything in her body was breaking.

Because sitting in the chair at the head of the table was the very man she'd left in bed only three hours before. *Dalton Chase.*

EVERY VOLUNTARY AND involuntary system in his body shut down at the sight of the two women standing at the opposite end of the table. One surprised him. The other delivered a heart-stopping shock. He couldn't breathe. He couldn't think. He couldn't move. He couldn't find his voice.

Cass Wheeler.

Time spun out, an intangible thing that became inconsequential as they simply stared at each other. Eric knew the others were watching the byplay, but it didn't matter. What mattered was what was happening between him and Cass right now. Everything they'd built was crumbling. He could see it in Cass's face. Salvaging it seemed both supremely important and simply impossible. So he sat there, mute with shock, and watched her slowly reanimate.

"G-Gentlemen," she stuttered. "If you'll excuse me for just a moment." Turning unsteadily in her heels, she slipped out of the conference room door before anyone said anything.

Gwen shot him a go-to-hell glare before nodding to the room in general and following Cass.

Eric didn't say anything. He couldn't. Not yet. He wanted to go to her, to explain he'd used a stage name, that he hadn't intentionally misled her, that he'd had no idea she was going to show up here today. Anything to stop her from bleeding out right in front of him.

Yet if he got out of his chair and went to Cass, he'd owe the board an explanation. That meant revealing his stripping venture. He couldn't risk alienating the conservatives in the group because he needed their financial backing to make this deal happen, even more so now with what Cass was about to present. Without their money, he was dead in the water.

The choice boiled down to Cass or his company, their future or the future of more than just two people. There was no right answer in this situation, and he knew it. People were going to be hurt. The question was, how many?

Eric wanted to throw something. Clenching his fists, he shifted his attention to the conversation when one of the board members addressed him directly.

"May I assume you have some relationship with this woman, Mr. Reeves?"

"I..." He stalled. What did he say? *She's my girlfriend, but she didn't know I was the head of this company until just now.* No. Just, no. He was willing to give these men his blood, sweat and tears. But they had no right to his dreams, and Cass was part of his dream for the future.

Clearing his throat, he continued. "I am. However, I didn't know she was the head of Preservations until just now. We weren't expecting to see each other in this venue."

"Clearly," one of the men said acerbically. "I'm going to have issues with funding this project if your personal life is going to interfere with our ability to move forward."

Eric bristled. Resting his forearms on the table, he glanced at every face. "I promise you nothing will affect our ability to get this project done with professionalism and visionary competence." The hard confidence in his voice left no room for doubt.

"You're certain?"

"I stayed in this room, didn't I?"

"Then someone please invite the women back in. I'd like to discuss this venture without further interference."

Eric pushed himself to stand at the same time the door opened.

Cass and Gwen entered the room, their movements smooth and graceful. Neither looked at him.

He couldn't stop staring. Cass was so beautiful, so incredibly composed, so—

Whurly placed his hands on the table, palms down and looked Cass over. "What does your father think of you working with his largest competitor, Ms. Jameson?"

—so very much David Jameson's daughter.

BARRAGED BY BATTLING EMOTIONS, Cass had no idea what to feel. She could only lift one shoulder in an approximation of a shrug. "My father has no more place in my professional business than I do in his, sir. Preservations operates on an ethical platform that doesn't allow me to discuss projects with anyone outside of the project's team."

"Young people don't understand ethics," the man countered.

"Then consider me an old soul. Preservations has never once been accused of improper behavior or compromised ethics, and it never will, *sir.*"

The words sounded hollow even to her ears, but apparently it pleased the codger considering her over the rim of his glasses.

"Then let's get on with this. Whatever it is between you and Mr. Reeves will be sorted out, I assume?"

"Allow me to be direct. There's nothing to sort out." She couldn't look at Dalton—*Eric*—no matter how much she wanted to. The urge to tear him down right where he sat was almost more than she could stand. It was the soul-wrenching devastation of betrayal that kept her silent.

He hadn't reacted to the announcement she was a Jameson, so he must have known. Had that been his plan? To keep her close, maybe seduce her, to ensure the plans, *his* plans, went through? Marcus's words came back to her, filling her head with the sounds of his mocking laughter. "Just remember that I warned you when this all blows up in your, face," he'd said. Well, it had blown up spectacularly.

She'd been played, a pawn in another man's game. But she was no one's throw-away piece.

17

ERIC NEARLY CAME OUT OF his chair when Cass said there was nothing to sort out. Like hell. She was Jameson's daughter. She'd been in his bed, in his life. Had she chosen him, singled him out, to get information on the project? Or had her desire for him been sincere? Confusion and fury wrestled in his mind, bouncing off the inside of his skull like sumo wrestlers.

He made it through the presentation without losing it, but it was a near thing several times. Cass and Gwen had done an admittedly stellar job outlining the EPA's requirements, Preservations' proposed solutions and the EPA's acceptance of the same. The problem? Their solutions exceeded his budget by more than $1.5 million dollars. *Million. Dollars.* There was no objecting to their plan. The EPA had approved it. Any alternative solutions would have to be redesigned, which cost money. They'd have to be resubmitted, which cost him time. And time was money. Everything translated to money. And now he had to convince the board to give it to him.

Leaning forward, he dropped his forearms to his knees and focused on Whurly, pointedly avoiding looking at

Cass. "Gentlemen, as you can see, Preservations' proposed solutions exceed the budget we gave them—"

"You'll find our solutions are the most cost-effective method of managing the runoff for the entire resort compound, *Mr. Reeves*."

The way she said his name killed him. He'd longed to hear her say it since he met her, and the moment was ruined by the fury in her voice.

"Furthermore," she continued, "Chok's project managers agree this is the most feasible means of diverting runoff and preserving the nesting area of the trumpeter swans that borders the resort on the south and west sides. You and the board are well aware the swans are of particular concern because of their status on the Audubon Washington Vulnerable Birds List."

His head snapped up and their eyes locked. A heated battle was waged in seconds without a word being exchanged. There was anger. God save him, there was so much anger. What hurt worse was the open betrayal that sliced both ways. Didn't she see that he was trying to save the project and by default her plan?

"We're not as concerned with the swans as we are with the implications of your proposal on the budget," Bradington, one of the most conservative board members, said quietly. "If this is the best you can do, we may have to explore other options."

Cass leaned forward and planted her hands on the table. "I'd encourage you to do just that, but allow me to be very clear here. If you determine Preservations isn't the best fit for this job and you go to another firm, we'll gladly step aside. When we do, though, our plans go with us and we won't be available for another consult."

"Threatening this board isn't the best way to impress us, young lady."

Eric watched the byplay, noting how Gwen's eyes first widened at Cass's declaration and then narrowed at Bradington's demeaning response. He needed to salvage the moment, but which moment? He could focus on the board and secure the money or reassure Cass that he was on her side and salvage their relationship...a relationship that might have been founded in subterfuge. Had she really lied to him?

His heart stuttered, skipping a beat before taking up a hard-rock rhythm in his chest. *Bam, bam, bam, bam.* It was relentless, beating against his ribs until he was compelled to clear his throat and shift.

Sitting on Eric's left, Whurly leaned over. "Reeves?"

"It's fine," he muttered.

"You're young for health issues." The old man leaned closer. "Prime age for matters of the heart, though."

Eric glanced at him, surprised to see compassion on the man's face.

"I'm a member of the board, Eric, not Satan's right-hand man." Settling back in his chair, he turned his attention to watch Cass, currently doing battle with Bradington.

Matters of the heart. And wasn't that exactly what this was? Even if it was a wounded heart. His mind raced, replaying conversations and quiet moments between them, searching for a time she could have used him or the knowledge he had provided. The harder he searched his memory, the more desperate he became to prove to himself she'd lied to him. Hell, he'd settled for her having misled him in any way. But there was nothing to find. Nothing stood out as deceitful. In fact, he'd kept most of the details of his day job from her, leaving no doubt whose was the bigger deceit.

His gaze shot to her profile, so pale under the fluorescent lighting. Jaw tight, her eyes flared at almost everything Bradington threw at her. They were really going at it, but Eric hardly heard a word they said. Days ago, he'd realized he needed to let go of some of his responsibilities and trust other people, to trust Cass. He'd taken a small step in that direction, but he hadn't gone far enough, and that was why they were in this mess.

Bradington slammed a fist on the table and yanked Eric into the moment. Gwen, Cass and the older man were all standing now. The man leaned in, closing the gap between him and Cass until they were nearly nose to nose. Sweat dampened the hair at his temples. "You are, without a doubt, the most underhanded, deceiving person I've met, your father and his ilk included. You think you can come in here with your father's name and interest in this project at your back and drive up the profits for your company by padding the numbers. We'll not stand for it. You've no ethics, girl, and you've no hope of selling your little engineering venture as a class act. Word will get out that you're on the take. That will be sufficient to see you to the same end your father should have found early on." Spittle flew from his lips with the final declaration.

"You seem to have an issue with my father, Mr. Bradington. That shouldn't translate to an issue with me or my firm." Cass's words were delivered softly with an undertone of sharp-edged steel. "I am not, and will never be, David Jameson."

"You are the very image of him, from your arrogance to your low-cut business suit. You assume Sovereign's board will simply roll over for you because you're a pretty face. You use your body instead of your brains to sell your product. It's despicable."

Eric shot out of his chair, sending it careening into

the wall with a crash loud enough to garner everyone's attention.

"About damn time," Mr. Whurly said under his breath.

Eric didn't spare him a glance. "You," he commanded, pointing at Gwen but looking at Bradington. "Sit."

Gwen's hands went to her hips and fire sparked in her eyes. "I'm not your—"

"Sit!" he roared.

Gwen took her seat, every movement slow and precise, and watched him from under a furrowed brow.

"And you," he said, turning to Cass, "come here." He pointed to his side.

She shook her head.

"Cass." The warning was clear.

"I told you, I don't appreciate being given orders and you *promised*—"

That her voice quavered now, here, in front of everyone, when he knew she'd fought through hell to keep her composure, ripped at his heart. "It got…complicated. Quickly. I didn't expect that."

"Me, either." A harsh laugh sounded torn from her throat. "I didn't even ask about your day job, Dal—Eric." She looked down and took a deep breath before meeting his gaze head-on. "I never pressed because it didn't occur to me you'd do anything of this magnitude."

Her admission stung. "You thought I wasn't capable?"

"No," she answered quickly. "Not that. It was my own prejudice. I never looked beyond the man in my…" She swallowed audibly. "The man in my arms." Shrugging, she crossed her arms under her breasts. "I'm not affiliated with my father, Eric. I didn't bring that into your house."

Bradington stood and crossed his arms. "You certainly don't believe this utter tripe."

"Sit. Down." Eric glared at the man until he sat again.

Then he looked back at Cass. "I know. I know this had, or has, nothing to do with your father. You were on my side, and I'm on yours."

Seeing her reaction, understanding how strongly she felt about her family, how she'd wanted to distance herself and be her own person, make her own way and earn her own scars—he was sure she hadn't betrayed him. He knew her; she was the person who had accepted him when even he hadn't. And now? He was done hiding, he was done being ashamed. Yes, he knew her; she was his dream, and his future.

Now all he had to do was prove it to her.

CASS FORCED HER BREATHING to slow down before she lifted her face to meet Eric's gaze.

He held out his hand to her. "Come here, Cass."

"I can't." It wasn't that she didn't want to go to him. She did. But she questioned whether or not her legs were going to hold her. Her knees were threatening to buckle, and, the longer she stood there, the more convinced she was they were going to let go. Then there was the matter of her pride. "You lied to me," she said. "That doesn't change, no matter what we wanted from each other."

His eyes flared, his hunger for her shining bright. "And what do you want, Cass?"

It didn't slip her notice he'd switched "wanted" to "want," keeping it in the present tense. Her gaze flew around the room, lighting on the faces ping-ponging back and forth between them. "Here?" she squeaked. "You want to do this here?"

"No more secrets."

"This room was built on secrets. Your downfall isn't going to be on my shoulders." She managed to take a step back.

"You're right. But that's about to change." He glanced around the table, and Cass watched a variety of emotions play across is face. "Gentlemen, I've been moonlighting for a number of years."

"Stop." She didn't want it to end this way, with him finally owning who he was and then watching her walk away. It was bad enough they were through, but to allow him to destroy himself like this? It was too much. "Eric, don't."

"It's fine. I have an ethics clause in my contract, and if Bradington thinks, however erroneously, that you're using your body for cash advantage, he should know I'm doing the same, without a doubt. And I'm not ashamed of it."

She started to shake. He was there, at her side, in between heartbeats, folding her into his arms.

"Please, I don't want you to be humiliated." She closed her eyes against the angry tears. "And neither do I. You don't need to tell them you used me."

His arms tightened around her "Used…you…" He cleared his throat. "Care to explain how you came to that conclusion?"

"You knew I was a Jameson, didn't you? You pursued me to keep my father off balance."

His whole body stiffened. Hurt and anger radiated off him, a fine vibration she felt along her skin an instant before he let her go and stepped away. "I assure you I had no idea you were related to David Jameson, and I apologize if you believe that's what the past six days were about, Ms. Wheeler."

Ms. Wheeler. It was over then. A very small part of Cass basked in the knowledge she'd been right, it had been too good to last. The rest of her wanted to weep.

Mr. Whurly rapped on the table, gaining everyone's attention. "You'll have to excuse me, Ms. Wheeler, because I'm not tracking most of this bizarre conversation. You and Mr. Reeves were involved, clearly. For how long?"

"I don't understand how that is relevant, sir." She locked her shaking knees, knowing what she was about to say would be a major setback to her company and her people. "I believe it's in our mutual interests if Preservations withdraws its proposal and allows Sovereign Developments to pursue other avenues of environmental management."

"Oh, nonsense," the older man answered, waving her off.

"Excuse me?"

"You heard me. Now, how long have you and Reeves been involved?"

"It's really none of your concern," she said, sure her cold delivery would shut him down.

He arched a brow, calm and unconcerned. "My investment firm has approximately thirty-five million dollars tied up in this project. I have the ability to fork out the nearly two million you need to manage runoff the way you'd like. I'd say that gives me a right to ask just about anything I want to know."

"I withdrew my services."

"Bullshit. You're punishing Reeves. Now, I want an answer. How long have you two been involved?"

She jerked at the sharp tone and answered instinctively. "A week."

"All this over a week?" Whurly shook his head. "You two must have something pretty powerful to warrant this much insanity so early in the relationship."

"There's no relationship," Cass asserted. "Not anymore."

"I'm going to call bullshit again, dear lady." To Bradington, he snapped, "Get out, Davis. You're off the project."

"You've no right to dismiss me," the other man declared piously.

"The hell I don't. I'll be taking your share of this daytime drama off your hands."

"It's not for sale."

"It will be. Now leave." Turning away from Bradington, Whurly—and every other board member—refocused on her. "What's so broken it can't be fixed so that you two can work together?" She looked at Eric, but Whurly snapped his fingers. "You'll answer me."

Cass's ire snapped into place, one vertebra at a time as it climbed her spine until she was ramrod straight, her hands fisted at her sides. "And you'll excuse me if I don't respond as a 'little lady' should. I've spent a lifetime being bullied by your kind, Mr. Whurly. It takes more than a snap of your fingers to impress me."

He chuckled before coughing into a handkerchief. "I knew I liked you." Watery eyes that were still sharp and clear met her stare head-on. "So what's so broken, Ms. Wheeler-Jameson?"

"Mr. Reeves deceived me, sir. I'll tolerate a great deal, but betrayal isn't on the list."

"And what did he lie to you about?"

"His name," she murmured. She might be through with Eric, but that didn't mean she was going to out him in front of the board of directors as an exotic dancer.

"And who, then, is Mr. Reeves?" Whurly asked, glancing curiously over her shoulder where Eric still hovered, the heat of him burning into her back.

"That's for him to disclose."

"Mr. Reeves?"

"My middle name is Dalton. My mother's maiden

name was Chase. So the name I gave her was Dalton Chase. It's all part of who I am, Cass. That wasn't a lie," Eric said quietly to her back. The words swept over her skin, the emotion in them twining with her own.

Whurly shifted in his seat so he could meet Eric's eyes. "Why bother with an alias?"

Eric tugged at his collar and whipped his chin to the side, popping his neck. "It has to do with my second job." He closed his eyes, let go of his collar and rose to his full height. Opening his eyes, he stared straight at Cass when he said, "I'm an exotic dancer at Beaux Hommes, Mr. Whurly. It's my primary source of income as I fight like hell to get Sovereign Developments into the black."

A couple of the board members pushed back in their chairs, crossing their arms over their chests and looking on with clear disdain.

"Bunch of ultraconservative idiots," Whurly muttered, waving them off.

Among the roiling emotional stew brewing in her belly, pride simmered closest to the surface. He'd done it. Eric had truly owned who he was. She knew what it had cost him to put himself out there like that. And wasn't that why she was hurt? Because she'd done the same, made herself vulnerable to him, and he'd promised not to use that against her? But how, exactly, had he used her? He'd never asked her for any information on her father, and she'd always gone by Wheeler. His deception had nothing to do with her, and if she held on to her sense of betrayal and closed herself off from his love, she would only allow her father to win. And Eric had shown her that that wasn't who she was.

She whirled toward him, and he automatically caught her. She planted her hands on his chest and stared up into the clearest green eyes she'd ever seen. He stared down at her, his gaze searching hers. He traced finger-tips along her jaw.

"I had no idea you were Jameson's daughter, Cass."

"I don't want to be," she admitted.

"It changes nothing about who we are, particularly after hours, though I suppose family dinners could be uncomfortable." One corner of his mouth lifted in a sardonic smile. "But you don't eat anyway. During the day?" He grinned full-on. "We're going to have to navigate the pros and cons of working together. I'll find the money and we'll move forward. That or I'll start looking for the next deal that will make Sovereign solvent." His face grew solemn. "I'll have to keep stripping until I can make it come together. But you come first, whatever it takes."

"Oh, keep your clothes on, son." Whurly stood and slapped him on the back. "It's been a long time since I've seen someone with your business savvy and sheer, unadulterated drive. I'll talk to the partners at my firm and we'll come up with the extra funds—even *after* we buy out Bradington."

Another man rose. "I'll agree to lending more money to the project. Any man willing to go to such degrees for the things he cares about is a man worth partnering with."

A few of the other men nodded and they all stood and shook hands as they left the boardroom.

Eric turned back to her, eyes wide. "Tell me that just happened."

"It just happened," she said, laughing.

A small, distinctly feminine cough interrupted whatever Eric might have said next. Gwen looked him over appraisingly. "You've got balls, Reeves, I'll give you that. But if you hurt her? I'll saw those balls off with the tines of a spork and feed them to my Rottweiler, Diesel."

Eric nodded solemnly. "Like I said, you're a terrifying wisp of a woman."

"As long as you don't forget it, we'll never have to find out how terrifying I can be. You'd be a bed-wetter when I was done with you." She grabbed her briefcase and the truck keys and started for the door. "I'm going back to the office to tell everyone the plan is a go and deal with the mole. You guys sort out whatever you have to sort out. I'll see you Saturday, Eric." Clicking the lock into place, she shut the door behind her.

"Saturday?" he asked Cass.

Cass smiled at Eric. "The wedding."

"Does that mean I'm forgiven?"

"Gwen is a complicated wisp."

"Clearly." He tucked his hands in his pockets. "Where were we before all—" he tipped his head toward the door "— *that?*"

"I think we were somewhere around 'where does this leave us?'"

"Right." Cupping her face, he leaned forward. "I believe this is the beginning of us, Cass, not the end."

She nodded slightly. "I do, too."

"Show me."

18

HE KISSED HER TENDERLY, his lips little more than a whisper across hers. His thumbs traced the planes of her cheeks as he tilted her head to the side slightly and took the kiss deeper.

Everything she felt for him rose to the surface in a rush, drowning out any doubt that had remained in the revelation of her love. Wrapping her arms around his neck, she pulled him closer.

The kiss seemed endless as they found their way back to each other. His teeth nipped her lips, then his tongue soothed the little bites as he murmured small words of passion to her.

Without warning, he took her hand and twirled her away from him.

She reached the end of their arms' length and laughed. "What was that for?"

"A reminder." He pulled her in close, wrapping his arms around her and settling his lips against the shell of her ear. "Mostly because I can't do a dramatic lift. But also because we don't have an aisle and backup dancers."

"An aisle and backup dancers?"

"Or a choreographer."

"You've gone over the edge, haven't you?"

"'Nobody puts Baby in the corner.' No one. Particularly the man who loves her."

Her breath caught.

He watched her closely, his gaze roaming over her face. "Say something, Cassidy. Please."

There was only one thing she could say, one truth she could give him unequivocally in that moment. "I love you, too, Eric Dalton Reeves."

He tightened his arms and lifted her, crushing his mouth to hers.

She rained kisses all over his face as he fervently whispered, "I love you, Cass. I swear I do. It's too soon, but I know it. I *know*. You're the one."

Their mouths came together in a rush of need, tongues tangling as they tasted each other. He'd had a peppermint at some point, she realized. An Altoid, given the potency of the flavor that lay over the coffee he'd had earlier. He smelled like fabric softener and salty air. The skin along his jaw was rough on her lips even though he'd clearly shaved.

"Dull razor," she murmured, licking the line of his jaw to his ear, where she nipped.

"Miserably dull. I couldn't afford a new..." He pulled away, brows creased. "Full disclosure, Cass. Just so there aren't any other misunderstandings."

Butterflies tumbled through her stomach, one after another. "What is it?"

"I'm busted-ass broke."

"Okay."

"No, Cass. Listen. I'm talking 'bounced my little brother's tuition check' broke." He looked away, color staining his cheeks. "I don't have much to offer. I don't want a dime from your family. That's not what this is

about. In fact, I don't want to be affiliated with your father at all except as the man who loves his daughter. It's
important that you understand—"

She kissed him. Hard. "Shut up," she whispered
against his mouth. "It doesn't matter, Eric."

"How can it not?" he persisted, pulling away to stare
down at her, puzzled.

"If you want to strip, strip. If you want to work at KFC,
I happen to love fried chicken. It doesn't matter because
it doesn't define you or our relationship. Besides, I might
have a way you can make a bit of extra cash."

She began backing toward the conference room table.
Eric's eyes widened, and Cass couldn't contain her grin.
"A thousand bucks says you take me on the table before
I'm done with you."

"I'm not wagering with you, Cass," he growled, his
eyes roaming over her body in that proprietary way that
made her shiver. The broad length of his arousal thick-
ened beneath the wool-and-silk blend of his trousers.

She grabbed his belt and pulled him along with her
as she continued to move toward the table. Once there,
she turned him around, parking his ass against the edge.
His hair was like silk slipping through her fingers as she
cupped his head and pulled him down for a kiss. Her free
hand ran his zipper down so she could work his swell-
ing erection through the opening of first his boxers and
then his pants. As she stroked him from root to tip, he
groaned into her mouth.

"Shh," she whispered. "You can't be loud."

"I'm not the loud one."

"You go on believing that, stud."

Her hand moved over the corona and he shivered.
"Damn it, Cass."

"If you want to win the bet, you're going to have to

do better than that." Dropping to her knees, she took his arousal between her lips and sank down on him. Working him with her hands and mouth, she quickly pushed him to the point his hips were thrusting of their own volition. His fingers tunneled into her hair, pins popping out and waves falling free as he held on. She watched as, lips parted, his head fell back. He was lost to her and she knew it, just as much as she knew she was lost to him.

Without warning, he hauled her up the front of his body and crushed his mouth to hers. The kiss stole her breath, a small mewl escaping.

"Shh," he teased.

"Eric," she said on a soft moan.

"Say it again."

Her brows drew together.

"My name, Cass. I want to hear my name on your lips, only ever my name."

"Eric," she breathed, hooking one leg around him and pulling him closer as he turned and maneuvered her onto the boardroom table. His strong, capable hands traced over her hips, bunching her skirt up to reveal the lingerie she'd chosen with him in mind only this morning. It seemed like ages ago.

Her head fell back, exposing her neck.

He moved his lips down to the place where neck and shoulder joined and bit her there softly.

She moaned. "What about the employees?"

"We're at the end of the office, empty offices on each side. And Gwen locked the door on her way out."

"Remind me to thank her," Cass gasped, pulling at his shirt.

He rapidly unbuttoned her blazer and leaned forward, suckling one pearled nipple through the silk of her bra. Sensation rocked her and sent a wave of heat through her that settled deep in her pelvis with a throbbing ache. She needed him. Now. No waiting.

"Holy Nutella," he breathed, staring down at her. "You wore garters and a thong."

"You said we'd be having lunch later."

He automatically glanced at the wall. "It's almost noon."

"Thank goodness," she said, arching one brow.

The broad head of his cock pushed at her, and she hooked her other leg around his waist, opening herself to him more fully.

With steady pressure, he worked his way in, his eyes never leaving hers. "I love you, Cass."

"I love you, too, Eric."

He began to move, slowly at first, then more aggressively, until she was forced to grip the edge of the table to keep from being pushed across its surface. Papers rained to the ground, an erotic chorus to their small sounds and whispered words of love.

Reaching between them, he found her clit and strummed the little bundle of nerves, gently at first and then faster. Her orgasm rolled over her and dragged her under. She couldn't see, couldn't breathe, couldn't hear and didn't care. Wave after wave of pleasure rocked her as he refused to let up on the pressure on her clit until a second orgasm took her and she cried out.

He followed her over the edge, burying his face in her neck to muffle his shout.

Eric was pretty sure he'd died. No one's heart could beat this fast and not suffer some kind of heart attack or stroke or something, he was sure. Chest heaving, he lay across Cass's prone body, listening to her gasping breaths and reveling in the way her fingers traced back and forth across his scalp. It was moments like these when he felt the true depth of his love for her. He'd been too scared to see it before now. Not anymore and never again. He was going to spend a lifetime making sure Cass always knew how much she was loved.

Pushing up so he rested on his elbows, he stared at her. "This is all your fault."

Her brow furrowed. "My fault?"

"It was those damn garters. I lost my head over the garters. I demand a rematch."

She laughed, her eyes saying all the things he needed to hear. "You won the bet, silly. Besides, the door handle to my office is broken."

"Maybe on a bulldozer on the construction site, then."

"You have something to tell me? Like, 'Hi, my name is Eric Reeves, and I'm an exhibitionist'?" she asked through her laughter.

"Cute. I was thinking we'd sneak out there after hours. You know—consecrate the site."

"Completely altruistic once again."

"Never let it be said I'm not a company man."

She snorted. "You own the company."

"I do, don't I? Well, at least I'm dedicated to its success."

"Absolutely." She pushed at his shoulder, still grinning. "Now, get off me so I can set myself to rights and we can get out of here while your employees are at lunch."

"Uh…about that." He felt the heat burn up his neck and across his cheeks.

"What?" she hissed, wiggling her skirt down around her lush hips.

"They take staggered lunches."

"So they're *out there?*" she squeaked, eyes wide, hands frozen over the buttons on her blazer.

"Yup. And my assistant only goes to lunch when I do, so we'll have to walk right by her."

"Where the hell did you find all these dedicated people?" she whispered, finger-combing her hair.

"Same place you found yours. 1-800-LOY-ALTY. They aren't the cheapest supplier, but their casualty rate is lowest among all the employee mills."

She gaped at him. "Your sense of humor is sick, you know that?"

He grinned. "Almost as sick as yours. Gives me something to aspire to."

Her bark of laughter was extraordinarily loud in the empty room. "True. It's just one more reason I love you."

Pulling her close, he fed his fingers through her hair and tilted her face up to his. "I'll never tire of hearing you say that any more than I'll ever stop trying to be worthy of it."

Eyes bright with emotion, she nodded. "Ditto." The rough timbre of her voice said she'd been caught off guard.

Good. He wanted to surprise her with something new every day from now on.

"Now, let's get out of here while the walk of shame is least populated."

She nodded, bending to pick up her hairpins.

"Leave them, baby. The cleaning company can manage that much."

"But they'll wonder."

"Let them." He held out his hand, his heart aching when she came to him without question and took what he offered. "Ready?"

"As I'll ever be."

They started down the hall, passing desks and offices, some empty and others occupied. No one said anything until they hit his office. His assistant sat out front, as predicted. The summer college intern was going over policy and procedure with her when they both looked up.

"Eric," she said, her mouth twitching. "It seems we should check the temperature controls in the conference room. You're a bit flushed."

"Your review is coming up, Gretchen. Keep that in mind," he said drily.

"Uh-huh." She smiled wide and winked at Cass. "Enjoy your lunch, you two."

Eric hauled Cass toward the exit, but she still heard the intern ask, "Wasn't her hair up when you showed her in earlier?"

"Shush, fledgling," Gretchen murmured. "You're young yet, but someday you'll learn that recognizing love is more important than picking out the details."

* * * * *

Don't miss Justin's story, the next revealing book in the PLEASURE BEFORE BUSINESS *series!*

#815 WICKED NIGHTS
Uniformly Hot!
by Anne Marsh
When local bad boy SEAL Cal Brennan threatens to put
Piper Clark's dive shop out of business, she'll do anything to
take him down a notch. Including proposing a sexy bet where
the loser takes orders from the winner for one night...in bed.

#816 SOME LIKE IT HOTTER
by Isabel Sharpe
California free-spirit Eva and her Manhattan sophisticate twin
sister agree to swap coasts and coffee shops—to perk things
up. When busy exec Ames Bradford makes stopping by a
nightly habit, Eva's soon brewing it up hot and satisfying!

#817 CLOSE UP
From Every Angle
by Erin McCarthy
Kristine Zimmerman is finally divorcing the man she left years
ago. Sean Maddock is even hotter now but there's nothing left
between them, right? Then he proposes a deliciously sinful
weekend for old times' sake...and she can't think of a single
reason to refuse.

#818 TRIPLE THREAT
The Art of Seduction
by Regina Kyle
Playwright Holly Ryan's Broadway dream may come true with
the help of sexy blockbuster star—and former high school
crush—Nick Damone. The heat and intensity between them
might set the stage on fire!

———————

HBCNM0914

REQUEST YOUR FREE BOOKS!
2 FREE NOVELS PLUS 2 FREE GIFTS!

HARLEQUIN®

Blaze®

red-hot reads!

YES! Please send me 2 FREE Harlequin® Blaze™ novels and my 2 FREE gifts (gifts are worth about $10). After receiving them, if I don't wish to receive any more books, I can return the shipping statement marked "cancel." If I don't cancel, I will receive 4 brand-new novels every month and be billed just $4.74 per book in the U.S. or $4.96 per book in Canada. That's a savings of at least 14% off the cover price. It's quite a bargain. Shipping and handling is just 50¢ per book in the U.S. and 75¢ per book in Canada.* I understand that accepting the 2 free books and gifts places me under no obligation to buy anything. I can always return a shipment and cancel at any time. Even if I never buy another book, the two free books and gifts are mine to keep forever.

150/350 HDN F4WC

Name _____ (PLEASE PRINT) _____

Address _____ Apt. # _____

City _____ State/Prov. _____ Zip/Postal Code _____

Signature (if under 18, a parent or guardian must sign) _____

Mail to the Harlequin® Reader Service:
IN U.S.A.: P.O. Box 1867, Buffalo, NY 14240-1867
IN CANADA: P.O. Box 609, Fort Erie, Ontario L2A 5X3

Want to try two free books from another line?
Call 1-800-873-8635 or visit www.ReaderService.com.

* Terms and prices subject to change without notice. Prices do not include applicable taxes. Sales tax applicable in N.Y. Canadian residents will be charged applicable taxes. Offer not valid in Quebec. This offer is limited to one order per household. Not valid for current subscribers to Harlequin Blaze books. All orders subject to credit approval. Credit or debit balances in a customer's account(s) may be offset by any other outstanding balance owed by or to the customer. Please allow 4 to 6 weeks for delivery. Offer available while quantities last.

Your Privacy—The Harlequin® Reader Service is committed to protecting your privacy. Our Privacy Policy is available online at www.ReaderService.com or upon request from the Harlequin Reader Service.

We make a portion of our mailing list available to reputable third parties that offer products we believe may interest you. If you prefer that we not exchange your name with third parties, or if you wish to clarify or modify your communication preferences, please visit us at www.ReaderService.com/consumerschoice or write to us at Harlequin Reader Service Preference Service, P.O. Box 9062, Buffalo, NY 14269. Include your complete name and address.

HB13R2

Piper was naked.

Okay, so she wasn't totally naked, but a man could dream.

Somehow, he'd timed his arrival at her slip for the precise moment she grabbed the zipper running up the back of her wet suit. Undeterred by his presence—because surely she'd heard him snap her name—she pulled, the neoprene suit parting slow and steady beneath her touch.

Hello.

Each new inch of sun-kissed skin she revealed made certain parts of him spring to life.

Even as he reminded himself that she'd spent most of their early days trying to either torment or kill him, however, his eyes were busy. Piper's arms were spectacular, strong and toned from hour after hour of pulling herself through the water and then back up into the boat. Now she was looking sexier than any stripper, uncovering skin that was a rich golden brown from time outdoors. The way she'd braided her water-slicked hair in a severe plait only drew his attention to the deceptively vulnerable curve of her neck.

But this was *Piper*.

So dragging his tongue over her skin and tasting all the

places where she was still damp from her dive should have been the *last* thing on his mind. He'd read her the riot act about her careless driving and say his piece about tomorrow's business meeting. Then he'd go his way and she'd go hers.

The wet suit hit her waist.

Neither short nor tall, Piper had medium-brown hair, brown eyes and a slim build. Those cut-and-dried facts didn't begin to do the woman in front of him justice, however. They certainly didn't begin to explain why he unexpectedly found her so appealing or why he wanted to wrap an arm around her and take her down to the deck for a kiss. Or seven. He didn't like Piper. He never had. She'd also made it plenty clear that he irritated her on a regular basis.

So why was he staring at her like a drowning man?

And…score another point for Piper. Like many divers, she hadn't bothered with a bikini top beneath the three-millimeter suit. His kiss quote rocketed up to double digits.

"Piper." His voice sounded hoarse to his own ears. *Focus.*

She jumped, her head swinging around toward him. "If it isn't my favorite SEAL."

Pick up WICKED NIGHTS
by *New York Times* bestselling author
Anne Marsh.

Available October 2014 wherever
you buy books and ebooks.

The EX Factor!

Kristine Zimmerman is finally divorcing the man she left years ago. Sean Maddock is even hotter now, but there's nothing left between them, right? Then he proposes a deliciously sinful weekend for old times' sake...and she can't think of a single reason to refuse!

From the reader-favorite

From Every Angle trilogy,

Close Up

by *Erin McCarthy*

Available October 2014 wherever you buy Harlequin Blaze books.

And don't miss

Double Exposure,

the first in the

From Every Angle trilogy, already available!

Red-Hot Reads

www.Harlequin.com

HB79821